RETURN TO THE SOURCE

*"I am a simple African man, doing my duty
in my own country in the context of our time."*

AMILCAR CABRAL
1924-1973

in memoriam.

RETURN
TO THE
SOURCE

Selected Speeches by
Amilcar Cabral

edited by Africa Information Service

Monthly Review Press
New York and London
with Africa Information Service

Copyright © 1973 by Africa Information Service and the
African Party for the Independence of Guinea and the
Cape Verde Islands
All Rights Reserved

Library of Congress Cataloging in Publication Data

Cabral, Amilcar
Return to the source.
1. Guinea, Portuguese—Politics and government—Collected
works. 2. Nationalism—Guinea, Portuguese—Collected works.
3. Guerrillas—Guinea, Portuguese—Collected works. I. Title.
DT613.75.C32   1974   320.9′66′5702   74-7788
ISBN 0-85345-345-4

Monthly Review Press
146 West 29th street, Suite 6W
New York, NY 10001

Dedicated to the struggle

The Africa Information Service (AIS) is an organization of Africans, African-Caribbeans and African-Americans who share a commitment to Third World anti-imperialist struggles. We prepare, catalog, and distribute information on African liberation movements and on the struggles to achieve economic independence by the people in those parts of Africa recognized as independent political states. We also provide the people of Africa with information on various struggles being waged by Third World peoples in the Western Hemisphere. Africa is our focal point, but we recognize that the African struggles do not exist in isolation. They are themselves part of a larger movement by Third World peoples.

Our thanks to the comrades and organizations who made the printing of this book possible, including the Africana Studies and Research Center of Cornell University and the Women's Division of the United Methodist Church.
And above all our special appreciation to the militants of the African Party for the Independence of Guinea* and the Cape Verde Islands (PAIGC) for their assistance.

Proceeds from the sale of this book will be sent to the PAIGC.

---

* Throughout this book the English (Guinea) and Portuguese (Guine) spellings are used interchangably.

Contents

CAPE VERDE
ISLANDS

Guinea (Bissau)

Angola

CABINDA

Mozambique

Namibia
(SWA)

Zimbabwe
(Rhodesia)

Portuguese
Colonies in
Africa

South Africa

Other white minority
dominated countries

Introduction

The long and difficult struggle to free Africa from foreign domination has produced many heroic figures and will continue to produce many more. In some instances individuals who seemed to be unlikely candidates emerged as spokesmen for the masses of their people. Often these were individuals who rejected avenues of escape from the realities of their people and who elected instead to return to the source of their own being. In taking this step these individuals reaffirmed the right of their people to take their own place in history.

Amilcar Cabral is one such figure. And in the hearts of the people of the small West African country of Guinea (Bissau), he will remain a leader who helped them regain their identity and who was otherwise instrumental in the initial stages of the long and difficult process of national liberation.

Cabral is recognized as having been one of the world's outstanding political theoreticians. At the time of his assassination by Portuguese agents, on Jan. 20, 1973—Cabral, as Secretary-General of the African Party for the Independence of Guinea and the Cape Verde Islands (PAIGC), was also an outstanding *practitioner* of these political theories. He had the ability to translate abstract theories into the concrete realities of his people, and very often the realities of his people resulted in the formulation of new theories.

The specific conditions of colonialism in Guinea (Bissau)

and on the Cape Verde Islands were instrumental in the political development of Cabral. To his people, Portuguese colonialism meant a stagnant existence coupled with the absence of personal dignity and liberty. More than 99% of the population could not read or write. Sixty percent of the babies died before reaching the age of one year. Forty percent of the population suffered from sleeping sickness and almost everyone had some form of malaria. There were never more than 11 doctors for the entire rural population, or one doctor for every 45,000 Africans.

In an effort to control the African population, Portugal attempted to create a minimally educated class, the members of which were granted the "privilege" of serving Portugal's interests. They were told to disdain everything African and to revere everything European. However, even if they adopted these attitudes they were never really accepted by their masters. The myth of Portugal's multi-racial society came to be exposed for what it was—a tool for little Portugal's continued domination of vast stretches of Africa.

Cabral studied in Portugal with Africans from other Portuguese colonies. This was a restive period in the development of African nationalist movements. The colonial powers had been weakened by the Second World War. And Africans had heard these powers speak of democracy, liberty and human dignity—all of which were denied to the colonial subjects. Many Africans had even fought and died for the "liberty" of their colonial masters. However, in the process those who survived learned much about the world and themselves.

Cabral's contemporaries as a student included Agostinho Neto and Mario de Andrade (founding members of the Popular Movement for the Liberation of Angola-MPLA), and Eduardo Mondlane* and Marcelino dos Santos (founding members of the Mozambique Liberation Front-FRELIMO). These men all rejected Portugal's right to define the lives of African people and committed themselves to struggle for change. As students they strived to assert their national identities and subsequently they returned to their respective countries to participate in the process of national liberation.

---

* Mondlane was himself the victim of an assassination carried out by Portuguese agents on February 3, 1969.

All of them saw that their peoples' enemy was not simply poverty, disease, or lack of education; nor was it the Portuguese people or simply whites; rather, it was colonialism and its parent imperialism. Cabral articulated this view in stating:

"We are not fighting against the Portuguese people, against individual Portuguese or Portuguese families. Without ever confusing the people of Portugal and Portuguese colonialism, we have been forced to take up arms in order to extirpate from the soil of our African fatherland, the shameful Portuguese colonial domination." Declaration made on the release of three Portuguese soldiers taken prisoner by the PAIGC, March, 1968.

This definition of the enemy proved an important ideological starting point. From here revolutionary theories were formulated and put into practice which resulted in the liberation of almost 75 percent of the countryside of Guinea (Bissau) in less than ten years of revolutionary armed struggle.

At the time of Cabral's murder, Guinea (Bissau) had virtually become an independent state with most of its principal towns occupied by a foreign army. In his *Second Address At the United Nations,* Cabral presented an overview of the struggle from its earliest days and he described life in the liberated areas of his country. He described the process of national reconstruction in the face of continuous bombardments and attacks by Portuguese soldiers. And, he announced the successful completion of freely held elections for a new National Assembly.

With each passing day Portugal finds itself more and more isolated from the international community. Not even the death of Cabral can reverse the tide which is running against one of the world's last remaining colonial rulers. In his *New Year's Message,* Cabral called on the PAIGC to press foward and continue the work necessary to issue a formal declaration of the new and independent state—Guinea (Bissau). This declaration will be issued during 1973 and will raise the struggle against Portuguese colonialism to another level.

The selections contained in this work illustrate a vital part of the study, analysis and application which made it possible for the people of Guinea (Bissau), and their comrades in Mozambique and Angola, to achieve what they have achieved in the face of numerous difficulties. For example, in *Identity and Dignity in the Context of the National Liberation Struggle,*

11

RETURN TO THE SOURCE

Cabral discusses the "return to the source" as a political process rather than a cultural event.

He saw the process of returning to the source as being more difficult for those "native elites" who had lived in isolation from the "native masses" and developed feelings of frustration as a result of their ambiguous roles. Thus, he viewed movements which propounded strictly cultural or traditional views to be manifestations of the frustrations resulting from being isolated from the African reality.

Among the many truths left by Cabral, is the fact that the process of returning to the source is of no historical importance (and would in fact be political opportunism) unless it involves not only a contest against the foreign culture but also complete participation in the mass struggle against foreign political and economic domination.

Africa Information Service
July, 1973

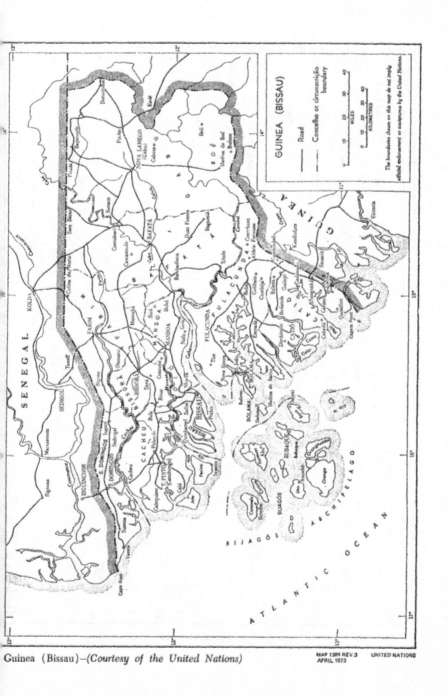

Guinea (Bissau)—*(Courtesy of the United Nations)*

MAP 1389 REV.3
APRIL 1973   UNITED NATIONS

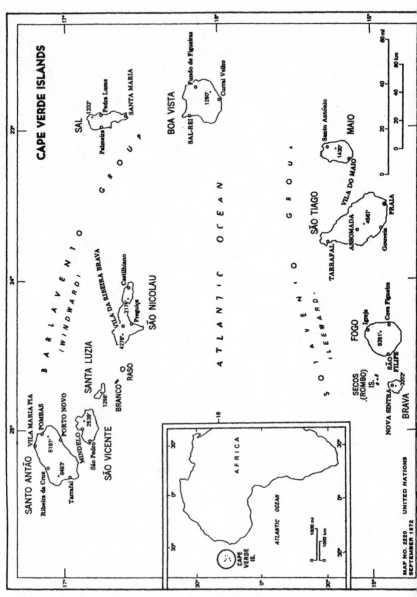

Cape Verde Islands—*(Courtesy of the United Nations)*

Second Address
Before
The United Nations

This speech was given during Amilcar Cabral's last visit to the United States. Presented before the Twenty-Seventh Session of the Fourth Committee of the United Nations General Assembly in New York, October 16, 1972, its contents were identified: "Questions of Territories under Portuguese Administration."

For the second time, I have the honor to address the Fourth Committee on behalf of the African people of Guine and the Cape Verde Islands, whose sole, legitimate, and true representative is the PAIGC. I do so with gratification, being fully aware that the members of the Committee are our comrades in the difficult but inspiring struggle for the liberation of peoples and mankind and against oppression of all kinds in the interest of a better life in a world of peace, security and progress.

While not forgetting the often remarkable role that Utopia could play in furthering human progress, the PAIGC is very realistic. We know that among members of the Fourth Committee, there are some who, perhaps in spite of themselves, are duty bound to adopt an obstructionist, if not negative attitude when dealing with problems relating to the struggle for national liberation in Guine and Cape Verde. I venture to say "in spite of themselves" because, leaving aside compelling reasons of State policy, it is difficult to believe that responsible men exist who

15

fundamentally oppose the legitimate aspirations of the African people to live in dignity, freedom, national independence and progress, because in the modern world, to support those who are suffering and fighting for their liberation, it is not necessary to be courageous; it is enough to be honest.

I addressed the Fourth Committee for the first time on 12 December 1962. Ten years is a long and even decisive period in the life of a human being, but a short interval in the history of a people. During that decade sweeping, radical and irreversible changes have occurred in the life of the people of Guine and Cape Verde. Unfortunately, it is impossible for me to refresh the memory of the members of the Committee in order to compare the situation of those days with the present, because most, if not all, of the representatives in the Committee are not the same. I will therefore briefly recapitulate the events up to the present.

On 3 August 1959, at a crucial juncture in the history of the struggle, the Portuguese colonialists committed the massacre of Pidgiguiti, in which the dock workers of Bissau and the river transport strikers were the victims and which, at a cost of 50 killed and over 100 strikers wounded, was a painful lesson for our people, who learned that there was no question of choosing between a peaceful struggle and armed combat; the Portuguese had weapons and were prepared to kill. At a secret meeting of the PAIGC leaders, held at Bissau on 19 September 1959, the decision was taken to suspend all peaceful representations to the authorities in the villages and to prepare for the armed struggle. For that purpose it was necessary to have a solid political base in the countryside. After three years of active and intensive mobilization and organization of the rural populations, PAIGC managed to create that basis in spite of the increasing vigilance of the colonial authorities.

Feeling the winds of change, the Portuguese colonialists launched an extensive campaign of police and military repression against the nationalist forces. In June, 1962, over 2,000 patriots were arrested throughout the country. Several villages were set on fire and their inhabitants massacred. Dozens of Africans were burnt alive or drowned in the rivers and others tortured. The policy of repression stiffened the people's determination to continue the fight. Some skirmishes broke out between the patriots and the forces of colonialist repression.

16

Faced with that situation, the patriots considered that only an appropriate and effective intervention by the United Nations in support of the inalienable rights of the people of Guine and the Cape Verde Islands could induce the Portuguese Government to respect international morality and legality. In light of subsequent events, we might well be considered to have been naive. We believed it to be our duty and right to have recourse to the international Organization. In the circumstances we considered it absolutely necessary to appeal to the Fourth Committee. Our message was the appeal of a people confronted with a particularly difficult situation but resolved to pay the price required to regain our dignity and freedom, as also proof of our trust in the strength of the principles and in the capacity for action of the United Nations.

What was the Fourth Committee told at that time? First of all, PAIGC clearly described the reasons for and purposes of its presence in the United Nations and explained that it had come as the representative of the African people of "Portuguese" Guine and the Cape Verde Islands. The people had placed their entire trust in PAIGC, an organization which had mobilized and organized them for the struggle for national liberation. The people had been gagged by the total lack of fundamental freedoms and by the Portuguese colonial repression. They considered those who had defended their interest in every possible way throughout the preceding 15 years of Africa's history to be their lawful representatives.

PAIGC had come to the Fourth Committee not to make propaganda or to extract resolutions condemning Portuguese colonialism, but to work with the Committee in order to arrive at a constructive solution of a problem which was both that of the people of Guine and Cape Verde and that of the United Nations itself: the immediate liberation of that people from the colonial yoke.

Nor had it come to inveigh against Portuguese colonialism, as had already been done many times—just as attacks had already been made and condemnations uttered against Portuguese colonialism, whose characteristics, subterfuges, methods and activities were already more than well known to the United Nations and world opinion.

PAIGC had come to the Fourth Committee because of the situation actually prevailing in our country and with the back-

17

ing of international law, in order to seek, together with the members of the Committee, including the Portuguese delegation, the shortest and most effective way of rapidly eliminating Portuguese colonialism from Guine and the Cape Verde Islands.

The time had come for our people and party to dispense with indecision and promises and to adopt definitive decisions and take specific action. We had already agreed to make great sacrifices and were determined to do much more to recover our liberty and human dignity, whatever the path to be followed.

It was not by chance that our presence in the Committee had not been considered indispensable until then. The legal, human and material requisites for action had not existed. In the course of the preceding years those requisites had been gradually accumulating, both for the United Nations and for the people engaged in the struggle, and PAIGC was convinced that the time had come to act and that the United Nations and the people of Guine and Cape Verde could really do so. PAIGC thought that, in order to act, it was necessary to establish close and effective co-operation and that it had the right and duty to help the United Nations so that it, in its turn, could help it to win back national freedom and independence. The help which PAIGC could provide had been mainly specific information on the situation in our country, a clear definition of the position adopted and the submission of specific proposals for a solution.

After describing the situation prevailing in the country, especially with regard to the intensified police and military repression, the fiction of the so-called "reforms" introduced by the Portuguese Government in September 1961 and the future prospects for our struggle, PAIGC analysed the problems relating to the legality or illegality of the struggle.

I will pass over some parts of that statement and confine myself to recalling that it was said that the resolution on decolonization not only imposed on Portugal and the people of Guine and Cape Verde the obligation to end colonial domination in that country but also committed the United Nations itself to take action in order to end colonial domination wherever it existed, with a view to facilitating the national independence of all colonial peoples. The people of Guine and Cape Verde were convinced that the Portuguese Government could not continue obstinately and with impunity to commit an international crime and that the United Nations had all the necessary means at its disposal for ordering and applying practical and effective measures designed to ensure respect for the principles of the Charter, impose international legality in our country and defend the interests of peace and civilization.

The representatives of the people of Guine and the Cape Verde Islands did not come to ask the United Nations to send troops to free our country from the Portuguese colonial yoke, because, even though it might have been able to do so, we did not think it necessary as we were sure of our ability to liberate our own country. We invoked the right to the collaboration and practical assistance of the United Nations with a view to expediting the liberation of our country from the colonial yoke and thus reducing the human and material losses which a protracted struggle might entail.

PAIGC was aware not only of the legality of our struggle but also of the fact that, fighting as we had been by all the means at our disposal for the liberation of our country, we had also been defending international legality, peace and the progress of mankind.

The struggle had ceased to be strictly national and had become international. In Guine and Cape Verde the fight for progress and freedom from poverty, suffering and oppression had been waged in various forms. While it was true that the victims of the fight had been the sons of the people of Guine and Cape Verde, it was also true that each comrade who had succumbed to torture or had fallen under the bullets of the Portuguese colonialists was identified—through the hope and conviction which the people of our country cherished in their hearts and minds—with all peace-loving and freedom-loving men who wished to live a life of progress in the pursuit of happiness.

In our country the fight had been waged not only to fulfill aspirations for freedom and national independence but also— and it would be continued until victory was won—to ensure respect for the resolutions and Charter of the United Nations. In the prisons, towns and fields of our country, a battle had been fought between the United Nations, which had demanded the elimination of the system of colonial domination of peoples, and the armed forces of the Portuguese Government which had sought to perpetuate the system in defiance of the people's legitimate rights.

The question had risen as to who was actually engaged in the fight. When a fighter had succumbed in our country to police torture, or had been murdered in prison, or burnt alive or machine-gunned by the Portuguese troops, for what cause had he given his life?

He had given his life for the liberation of our people from the colonial yoke and hence for the cause of the United Nations. In fighting and dying for the country's liberation, he had given his life, in a context of international legality, for the ideals set forth in the Charter and resolutions of the United Nations, especially for the resolution on decolonization.

For our people, the only difference between an Indian soldier, an Italian pilot or a Swedish official who had died in the Congo and the combatant who had died in Guine or the Cape Verde Islands was that the latter, fighting in his own country in the service of the same ideal, was no more than an anonymous combatant for the United Nations cause.

PAIGC believed that the time had come to take stock of the situation and make radical changes in it, since it benefited only the enemies of the United Nations and, more specifically, Portuguese colonialism.

We Africans, having rejected the idea of begging for freedom, which was contrary to our dignity and our sacred right to freedom and independence, reaffirmed our steadfast decision to end colonial domination of our country, no matter what the sacrifices involved, and to conquer for ourselves the opportunity to achieve in peace our own progress and happiness.

With that aim in view and on the basis of that irrevocable decision, PAIGC had defined three possible ways in which the conflict between the Government of Portugal and the African people might evolve and be resolved. Those three possibilities were the following: (a) a radical change in the position of the Portuguese Government; (b) immediate specific action by the United Nations; and (c) a struggle waged exclusively by the people with their own means.

As proof of its confidence in the Organization, and in view of the influence which some of the latter's Members could certainly exert on the Portuguese Government, PAIGC had taken into consideration only the first two possibilities and in that connection had submitted the following specific proposals:

(a) With regard to the first possibility:

The immediate establishment of contact between the Portuguese delegation and the PAIGC delegation;

Consultations with the Portuguese Government to set an early date for the beginning of negotiations between that Government's representatives and the lawful representatives of Guinea and the Cape Verde Islands;

Pending negotiations, suspension of repressive acts by the Portuguese colonial forces and of all action by the nationalists.

(b) With regard to the second possibility:

Acceptance of the principle that United Nations assistance would not be really effective unless it was simultaneously moral, political and material;

Immediate establishment within the United Nations of a special committee for the self-determination and national independence of the Territories under Portuguese administration;

Immediate commencement of that committee's work before the close of the General Assembly session.

PAIGC also stated that it was ready to co-operate fully with that committee and proposed that the latter should be entrusted with the task of giving concrete assistance to our people so that we could free ourselves speedily from the colonial yoke. Since those proposals were not favorably received by the Portuguese Government or the United Nations, the patriotic forces of our country launched a general struggle against the colonialist forces in January 1963 in order to respond, by an armed struggle for liberation, to the colonial genocidal war unleased against the people by the Government of Portugal.

Almost 10 years later, PAGIC is again appearing before the Fourth Committee. The situation is completely different, however, both within the country and at the international level. The Fourth Committee and the United Nations are now better informed than ever before about the situation. In addition to the current information (reports, information bulletins, war communiques and other documents which PAIGC has sent to the United Nations), PAIGC has, in those 10 years appeared before the Decolonization Committee to describe the progress of the struggle and prospects for its future evolution. Dozens of film-makers, journalists, politicians, scientists, writers, artists,

RETURN TO THE SOURCE

photographers, and so on of various nationalities have visited the country on their own initiative and at the invitaton of PAIGC and have provided unanimous and irrefutable testimony regarding the situation. Others—very few in number—have done the same on the colonialist side at the invitation of the Portuguese authorities and, with few exceptions, their testimony has not completely satisfied those authorities. For example, there was the case of the team from the French radio and television organization which visited all the "overseas provinces," and whose film was rejected by the Lisbon Government because of the part relating to Guine and Cape Verde. That film was shown to the Security Council in Addis Ababa. Another case was that of the group of representatives of the people of the United States, headed by Representative Charles Diggs, whose report on their visit to the country merits careful study by the Committee and anyone else wishing to obtain reliable information on the situation. However, the United Nations has at its disposal information which is, in our view, even more valuable, namely the report of the Special Mission which, at the invitation of PAIGC and duly authorized by the General Assembly, visited the liberated regions of the country in April 1972. I am not, therefore, appearing before the Committee to remedy a lack of information.

Furthermore, the United Nations and world opinion are sufficiently well informed about the crimes against African people committeed daily by the Portuguese colonialists. A number of victims of Portuguese police and military repression have testified before United Nations bodies, particularly the Commission on Human Rights. At the twenty-sixth session, two of my countrymen, one with third-degree napalm burns and the other with mutilated ears and obvious signs of torture appeared before the Committee. Those who have visited my country, including members of the United Nations Special Mission, have been able to see the horrifying consequences of the criminal acts of the Portuguese colonialists against the people and the material goods which are the fruits of their labour. Unfortunately the United Nations, like the African people, is well aware that condemnations and resolutions, no matter how great their moral and political value, will not compel the Portuguese Government to put and end to its crime of

22

lese-humanite*. Consequently, I am not appearing before the Committee in order to obtain more violent condemnations and resolutions against the Portuguese colonialists.

Nor am I urging that an appeal should be made to the allies of the Government of Portugal to cease giving it political suport and material, military, economic and financial assistance, which are factors of primary importance in the continuation of the Portuguese colonial war against Africa, since that has already been done on many past occasions with no positive results. It should be noted, not without regret, that I was right in stating almost 10 years previously that in view of the facts concerning the Portuguese economy and the interests of the States allied to the Government of Portugal, recommending or even demanding a diplomatic, economic and military boycott would not be an effective means of helping the African people. Experience has shown, on the contrary, that in acting or being forced to act as real enemies of the liberation and progress of the African peoples, the allies of the Portuguese Government and in particular some of the main NATO** Powers have not only increased their assistance to the Portuguese colonialists but have systematically avoided or even boycotted any co-operation with the United Nations majority which is seeking to determine legally the political and other steps which might induce the Government of Portugal to comply with the principles of the Organization and the resolutions of the General Assembly. It was not 10 years before but in recent years that the Government of Portugal has received from its allies the largest quantities of war material, jet aircraft, helicopters, gunboats, launches, and so on. It was in 1972, not 1962, that the Government of Portugal received some $500 million in financial assistance from one of its principal allies. If States which call themselves champions of freedom and democracy and defenders of the "free world" and the cause of self-determination and independence of peoples thus persist in supporting and giving practical assistance to the most retrograde colonialism on earth, they must have very good reasons, at least in their own view. Perhaps an effort should be made to understand them, even if their reasons are unavowed or unavowable. It is no doubt necessary to take a realistic approach and to stop dreaming and asking

---

* lese-humanite—against humanity
** North Atlantic Treaty Organization

23

the impossible, for as we Africans say, "only in stories is it possible to cross the river on the shoulders of the crocodile's friend."

I am appearing once more before the United Nations to try, as in the past, to obtain from the Organization practical and effective assistance for my struggling people. However, as I have already said and as everyone knows, the current situation is in every way very different from that obtaining in 1962, and the aid which the African people need is likewise different.

During almost 10 years of armed struggle and of enormous efforts and sacrifices, almost three quarters of the national territory has been freed from Portuguese colonial domination and two thirds brought under effective control, which means in concrete terms that in most of the country the people have a solid political organization— that of PAIGC–a developing administrative structure, a judicial structure, a new economy free from all exploitation of the people's labour, a variety of social and cultural services (health, hygiene, education) and other means of affirming their personality and their ability to shape their destiny and direct their own lives. They also have a military organization entirely composed of and led by sons of the people. The national forces, whose task is to attack the colonialist troops systematically wherever they might be, in order to complete the liberation of the country, like the local armed forces, which are responsible for the defence and security of the liberated areas, are now stronger than ever, tempered by almost 10 years of struggle. That is proved by the colonialists' inability to recover even the smallest part of the liberated areas by their increasingly heavy losses, and by the people's ability to deal them increasingly heavy blows, even in the main urban centres such as Bissau, the capital and Bafata, the country's second largest town.

For the people of Guine and Cape Verde and our national party, however, the greatest success of our struggle does not lie in the fact that we have fought victoriously against the Portuguese colonialist troops under extremely difficult conditions but rather in the fact that, while we were fighting, we began to create all the aspects of a new life—political, administrative, economic, social and cultural—in the liberated areas. It is, to be sure, still a very hard life, since it calls for great effort and sacifice in the face of a genocidal colonial war, but it is a life full of beauty, for it is one of productive, efficient work, freedom and democracy in which the people have regained their dignity. The nearly 10 years of struggle have not only forged a new, strong African nation but also created a new man and a new woman, people possessing an awareness of their rights and duties, on the soil of the African fatherland. Indeed, the most important result of the struggle, which is at the same time its greatest strength, is the new awareness of the country's men, women and children.

The people of Guine and Cape Verde do not take any great pride in the fact that every day, because of circumstances created and imposed by the Government of Portugal, an increasing number of young Portuguese are dying ingloriously before the withering fire of the freedom-fighters. What fills us with pride is our ever-increasing national consciousness, our unity—now indestructible—which has been forged in war, the harmonious development and coexistence of the various cultures and ethnic groups, the schools, hospitals and health centres which are operating openly in spite of the bombs and the terrorist attacks of the Portuguese colonialists, the people's stores which are increasingly able to supply the needs of the population, the increase and qualitative improvement in agricultural production, and the beauty, pride and dignity of our children and our women, who were the most exploited human beings in the country. We take pride in the fact that thousands of adults have been taught to read and write, that the rural inhabitants are receiving medicines that were never available to them before, that no fewer than 497 high- and middle-level civil servants and professional people have been trained, and that 495 young people are studying at higher, secondary and vocational educational establishments in friendly European countries while 15,000 children are attending 156 primary schools and five secondary boarding schools and semi-boarding schools with a staff of 251 teachers. This is the greatest victory of the people of Guine and Cape Verde over the Portuguese colonialists, for it is a victory over ignorance, fear and disease—evils imposed on the African inhabitants for more than a century by Portuguese colonialism.

It is also the clearest proof of the sovereignty enjoyed by the people of Guine and Cape Verde, who are free and sovereign in the greatest part of our national territory. To defend and preserve that sovereignty and expand it throughout the entire national territory, both on the continent and on the islands, the people have not only their armed forces but all the machinery of a State which, under the leadership of the party, is growing stronger and consolidating itself day by day. Indeed, the position of the people of Guine and Cape Verde has for some time been comparable to that of an independent State part of whose national territory—namely, the urban centres—is occupied by foreign military forces. Proof of that is the fact that for some years the people have no longer been subject to economic exploitation by the Portuguese colonialists, since the latter are no longer able to exploit them. The people of Guine and Cape Verde are all the more certain of gaining their freedom because of the fact that, both in the urban centres and in the occupied areas, the clandestine organization and political activities of the freedom-fighters are more vigorous than ever.

There is no force capable of preventing the complete liberation of my people and the attainment of national independence by my country. Nothing can destroy the unity of the African people of Guine and Cape Verde and our unshakable determination to free the entire national territory from the Portuguese colonial yoke and military occupation.

Confronted with that situation and that determination, what is the attitude of the Portuguese Government? Up until the death of Salazar, whose outmoded ways of thinking made it impossible for him to conceive of granting even fictitious concessions to the Africans there was talk only of radicalizing the colonial war. Salazar, who would repeat over and over to anyone willing to listen that "Africa does not exist" (an assertion which clearly reflected an insane racism but which also perfectly summed up the principles and practices which have always characterized Portuguese colonial policy), was at his advanced age unable to survive the affirmation of Africa's existence: the victorious armed resistance of the African peoples to the Portuguese colonial war. Salazar was nothing more than a fanatical believer in the doctrine of European superiority and African inferiority. As everyone knew, Africa was the sickness that killed Salazar.

Marcelo Caetano, his successor, is also a theoretician (professor of colonial law at the Lisbon School of Law) and a practical politician (Minister of Colonies for many years). Caetano, who claims that he "knows the blacks," has decided on a new policy which, in the sphere of social relationships, is to be that of a kind of master who holds out the hand of friendship to his "boy"; politically speaking the new policy is in its essence nothing more than the old tactic of force and deceit while outwardly it makes use of the arguments and even the actual words of the adversary in order to confuse him while actually maintaining the same position. That is the difference between the Salazarism of Salazar and the neo-Salazarism of Caetano. The objective remains the same: to perpetuate white domination of the black masses of Guine and Cape Verde.

Caetano's new tactic, which the people refer to as "the policy of smiling and bloodshed," is merely one more result and success of the struggle being waged by the Africans. That fact has been noted by many who have visited the remaining occupied areas of Guine and in Cape Verde, including the American Congressman, Charles Diggs, and it is also understood by the people of the occcupied areas who replied to the colonialists' demagogic concessions with the words "*Djarama*, PAIGC," i.e. "Thank you, PAIGC." In spite of those concessions and the launching of a vast propaganda campaign both in Africa and internationally, the new policy has failed. The people of the liberated areas are more united than ever around the national party, while those of the urban centres and the remaining occupied areas are supporting the party's struggle more strongly every day both in Guine and Cape Verde. Hundreds of young people are leaving the urban centres, especially Bissau, to join the fight. There are increasing desertions from the so-called *unidades africanas**, many of whose members are being held prisoner by the colonial authorities.

Confronted with that situation, the colonialists are resorting to increased repression in the occupied areas, particularly the cities, and stepping up the bombings and terrorist attacks against the liberated areas. Having been forced to recognize that they cannot win the war, they now know that no stratagem can demoralize the people of those areas and that nothing can halt our advance towards complete liberation and independence. They are therefore making extensive use of the means available to them and attempting at all costs to destroy as many lives and

---

* African mercenaries fighting for Portugal

as much property as they can. The colonialists are making increased use of napalm and are actively preparing to use toxic substances, herbicides and defoliants, of which they have large supplies in Bissau, against the freedom-fighters.

The Portuguese Government's desperation is all the more understandable because of the fact that the peoples of Angola and Mozambique are succeeding in their struggle and that the people of Portugal are becoming more strongly opposed to the colonial wars every day. In spite of appearances, Portugal's economic, political and social position is steadily deteriorating and the population declining, mainly because of the colonial wars. I wish to reaffirm my people's solidarity not only with the fraternal African peoples of Angola and Mozambique but also with the people of Portugal, whom my own people have never equated with Portuguese colonialism. My people are more convinced than ever that the struggle being waged in Guiné and Cape Verde and the complete liberation of that Territory will be in the best interests of the people of Portugal, with whom we wish to establish and develop the best possible relations on the basis of co-operation, solidarity and friendship in order to promote genuine progress in my country once it wins its independence.

Although the Portuguese Government has persisted in its absurd, inhuman policy of colonial war for almost 10 years, the United Nations has made a significant moral and political contribution to the progress of my people's liberation struggle. The resolutions proclaiming that it is legitimate to carry on that struggle by any means necessary, the appeal to Member States to extend all possible assistance to the African liberation movements, the recommendations to the specialized agencies to co-operate with those movements through OAU* the granting of hearings to their representatives at the Security Council meetings in Addis Ababa, the granting of observer status to certain liberation movements and, in my own case, the Special Mission's visit to my country and the recognition of my party by the Committee on Decolonization as the only legitimate, authentic representative of the people of Guiné and Cape Verde represented important assistance to those struggling peoples. We are grateful for the aid received, from the Commit-

---

* Organization of African Unity

tee on Decolonization and its dynamic Chairman, the Fourth
Committee and, through it, the General Assembly and all
Member States which are sympathetic to our cause.

Nevertheless, I do not feel that there is nothing more the
United Nations can do to aid my people's struggle. I am convinced that the Organization can and must do more to hasten
the end of the colonial war in my country and the complete
liberation of my people. I have for that reason submitted
specific proposals to the Security Council in Addis Ababa. Because of my confidence in the United Nations and in its ability
to take action in the specific case of Guine and Cape Verde,
I am now submitting new proposals aimed at the establishment
of closer, more effective co-operation between the Organization
and the national party, which is the legitimate representative
of the people of Guine and Cape Verde. Before doing so, I
would draw attention to some important events that have taken
place in my country in recent months.

I will not speak about the successes achieved by the freedom-
fighters during the past year, although they have been significant
ones. I will begin by referring to the United Nations Special
Mission's visit to my country, which was made in April despite
the terrorist aggression launched by the Portuguese colonialists
against the liberated south in an effort to prevent the visit from
taking place. An historic and unique landmark for the United
Nations and the liberation movements, the visit was unques-
tionably a great victory for my people but it was also one for
the international organization and for mankind. It provided
a new stimulus to the courage and determination of my people
and its fighters, who were willing to make sacrifices in order to
make it possible. While it is true that the findings of the Special
Mission merely added more evidence of the same kind as had
been given by many unimpeachably reliable visitors, various
professional persons and nationalists, they nevertheless have
special value and significance, since they are findings of the
United Nations itself, made by an official mission duly authorized by the General Assembly and consisting of respected representatives of three Member States. I emphasize the great
importance of the Special Mission's success, express my gratitude
to the General Assembly for authorizing it and to Ecuador,
Sweden and Tunisia for allowing their distinguished representatives, Mr. Horacio Sevilla Borja, Mr. Folke Lofgren and

29

Mr. Kamel Belkhira, to participate in it and again congratulate all the participants and Secretariat staff members on having performed with exemplary courage, determination and conscientiousness the duties of a historic and profoundly humanitarian assignment in the service of the United Nations and of the people of Guine and Cape Verde, and hence in the service of mankind.

Any action, regardless of its motives, is sterile unless it produces practical and concrete results. PAIGC's motive in inviting the United Nations to send a Special Mission to its country was not to prove the sovereignty of the people of Guine over vast areas of the country, a fact which was already clear to everyone; instead, it deliberately tried to give the United Nations another specific basis for taking effective measures against Portuguese colonialism. That basis has been established by the success of the Special Mission; it seems just and essential to take full advantage of it, since PAIGC, like the Special Mission, is convinced that the political situation of the people of Guine, including their legal situation, cannot remain as it has been in the past. PAIGC is also convinced that the United Nations will be able to implement the recommendations of the Special Mission and declares its readiness to extend whatever cooperation is needed to that end.

Like any important event, the Mission's success involved some amusing sidelights, such as the desperate and preposterous response expressed both orally and in writing by the Lisbon Government. In that connection I quote a proverb current among the people of Guine, "A person who spits at the sun succeeds only in dirtying his own face."

Another important event is the establishment of the first National Assembly of the people of Guine. Universal general elections have just been held by secret ballot in all the liberated areas for the purpose of forming regional councils and choosing the 120 representatives to the first National Assembly, 80 elected by the masses of the people and 40 chosen from among the members of the Party. The people of Guine and PAIGC are firmly resolved to take full advantage of the establishment of our new organs of sovereignty. The National Assembly will proclaim the existence of the State of Guine and give it an executive authority that will function within the country. In that connection, PAIGC is sure of the fraternal and active support of the independent African States and feels encouraged by the certainty that not only Africa but also the United Nations and all genuinely anti-colonialist States will fully appreciate the political and legal development of the situation in that African nation. In point of fact, at the present stage of the struggle the Government of Portugal neither can nor should represent the people of Guine either in the United Nations or in any other international organization or agency, just as it can never represent it in the OAU.

For that reason, PAIGC is not raising the question of calling for the expulsion of Portugal from the United Nations or from any other international organization. The real question is whether or not the people of Guine, who hold sovereignty over most of their national territory, and who have just formed their first National Assembly which is going to proclaim the existence of its State, headed by an executive authority, have the right to become a member of the international community within the framework of its organizations, even though part of its country is occupied by foreign military forces. The real question before the people of Guine, which has to be answered categorically, is whether the United Nations and all the anti-colonialist forces are prepared to strengthen their support and their moral, political and material assistance to that African nation as their specific capabilities permit.

It is true that the war is still ravaging the country and that the people will have to continue making sacrifices to win the liberation of their homeland. That has already happened and is happening in other places, to peoples which have a Government of their own and a standing in international law. But it is also true that, thanks to international solidarity, more and more resources (and more effective ones) are becoming available to the people of Guine, enabling them to deal harder blows to the Portuguese colonial troops, and that the people's determination and the valour and experience of our fighters are increasing day by day. The only reason why PAIGC does not trouble to declare that Portugal runs the risk of military defeat in Guine is that Portugal has never had any chance of victory, and for that reason too the people of Guine will continue to maintain our principles: peace, a search for dialogue and negotiation for the solution of our conflict with the Government of Portugal.

In the Cape Verde Islands, where hunger again reigns, while the colonialists are intensifying their oppression because of PAIGC's political activity, PAIGC is determined to promote the struggle by all necessary means in order to free the African people completely from the colonial yoke. Above all, PAIGC denounces the despicable efforts of the Government of Portugal to take advantage of the situation in the Islands by exporting workers to Portugal and other colonies in order to sap the people's strength and thus undermine our struggle. PAIGC wishes to reaffirm that, by reason of the community of blood, history, interests and struggle between the peoples of Guinea and the Islands, it is determined to make whatever sacrifices are necessary in order to liberate the Cape Verde archipelago from Portuguese domination.

I call to the attention of the United Nations through the Fourth Committee, the following proposals, based on the practical realities of the life of the people of Guine and on all the considerations I have just discussed:

1. Representations to the Government of Portugal for the immediate start of negotiations between the representatives of that Government and those of PAIGC. The programme of those negotiations should be based on a search for the most appropriate and effective means for the early attainment of independence by the people of Guine. If the Government of Portugal responds favourably to that initiative, PAIGC might consider ways of taking into account the interests of Portugal in Guine.

2. Immediate acceptance of PAIGC delegates, in the capacity of associate members or observers, in all the specialized agencies of the United Nations as the sole legitimate representatives of the people of Guine, as is already true in the case of ECA*.

3. Development of practical assistance from the specialized agencies, particularly UNESCO, WHO, FAO and UNICEF**, to the people of Guine, as a part of that country's national reconstruction. I hope that any undue legalistic or bureaucratic obstacles in that sphere can be overcome.

---

* Economic Commission for Africa
** United Nations Economic and Social Council, World Health Organization, Food and Agriculture Organization, United Nation Children's Emergency Fund.

4. Moral and political support by the United Nations for all initiatives that the people of Guine and the PAIGC have decided to adopt with a view to an early end of the Portuguese colonial war and to the achievement of that African country's independence in order that it might soon occupy its rightful place in the international community.

In the hope that those proposals will be given serious consideration, I strongly urge all Member States of the United Nations, in particular Portugal's allies, the Latin American countries and especially Brazil, to understand Guine's position and support that African people's legitimate aspirations to freedom, independence and progress. The Latin American countries have had to fight for their independence. Portugal often cites the case of Brazil as an example in favour of its position, even though a struggle for independence has taken place in Brazil as well. Portugal itself gained its freedom through a fratricidal struggle; the people of Guine however, have no family ties with the people of Portugal.

I thank the African countries, the socialist countries, the Nordic countries and all other countries and non-governmental organizations, such as the World Council of Churches, the World Church Services and the Rowntree Social Trust which are helping Guine in its struggle for liberation. At the same time, I do not believe that the attitude of States giving aid to Portugal reflects the feelings of most of their inhabitants. The people of Guine are certain of final victory and hope to establish co-operative and peaceful relations with all peoples. I thank the Committee for its welcome and reaffirm that I am at its disposal at any time.

Soldiers inside a liberated zone. (Liberation News Service)

A PAIGC soldier studying. (Liberation News Service)

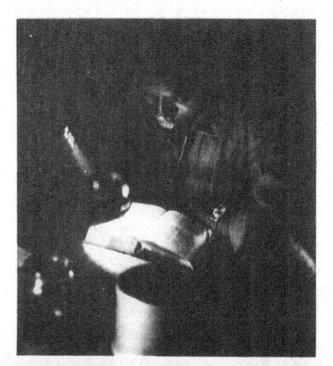

Soldiers at a military base in a liberated region of Guine. (Liberation News Service)

Students at a gymnasium class at the Aerolino Lopez Cruz boarding school located in the Cubucare Sector, Southern Zone, in liberated Guine. The school was named after the teacher who died while protecting the students during a Portuguese air raid in 1965. (UN Photo/Yutaka Nagata)

Members of the PAIGC are seen being inspected by an officer in the Cubucare Sector. (UN Photo/Yutaka Nagata)

On September 24, 1973 the Republic of Guine-Bissau was proclaimed. Some of the political leaders of the Republic are seen here at a meeting —far left: Chico Mendes, Prime Minister; center: Luis Cabral, President of the Council of State; right: Lucio Soares, commander of the Northern Front. (AIS/Robert Van Lierop)

Kitchen of a military encampment in a liberated zone. (Liberation News Service)

The office at a military encampment; here local military and political leaders meet. (Liberation News Service)

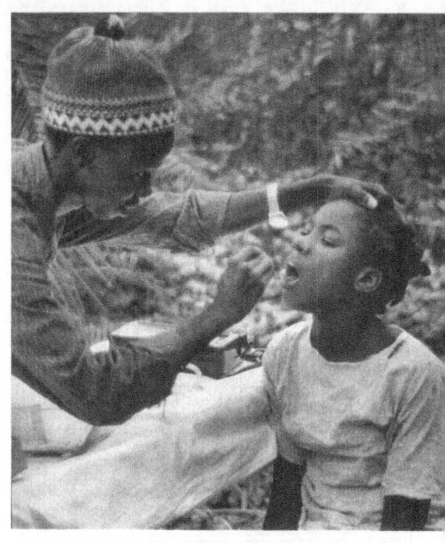

A young girl is examined by a male nurse at a health station near the village of Bcama. (AIS/Robert Van Lierop)

National Liberation
and Culture

This text was originally delivered on February 20, 1970, as part of the Eduardo Mondlane* Memorial Lecture Series at Syracuse University, Syracuse, New York, under the auspices of The Program of Eastern African Studies. It was translated from the French by Maureen Webster.

When Goebbels, the brain behind Nazi propaganda, heard culture being discussed, he brought out his revolver. That shows that the Nazis—who were and are the most tragic expression of imperialism and of its thirst for domination—even if they were all degenerates like Hitler, had a clear idea of the value of culture as a factor of resistance to foreign domination.

History teaches us that, in certain circumstances, it is very easy for the foreigner to impose his domination on a people. But it also teaches us that, whatever may be the material aspects of this domination, it can be maintained only by the permanent, organized repression of the cultural life of the people concerned. Implantation of foreign domination can be assured definitively only by physical liquidation of a significant part of the dominated population.

In fact, to take up arms to dominate a people is, above all, to take up arms to destroy, or at least to neutralize, to paralyze, its cultural life. For, with a strong indigenous cultural life, for-

---

* Eduardo Mondlane, was the first President of the Mozambique Liberation Front (FRELIMO). He was assassinated by Portuguese agents on Feb. 3, 1969.

eign domination cannot be sure of its perpetuation. A. any moment, depending on internal and external factors determining the evolution of the society in question, cultural resistance (indestructible) may take on new forms (political, economic, armed) in order fully to contest foreign domination.

The ideal for foreign domination, whether imperialist or not, would be to choose:

— either to liquidate practically all the population of the dominated country, thereby eliminating the possibilities for cultural resistance;

— or to succeed in imposing itself without damage to the culture of the dominated people—that is, to harmonize economic and political domination of these people with their cultural personality.

The first hypothesis implies genocide of the indigenous population and creates a void which empties foreign domination of its content and its object: the dominated people. The second hypothesis has not, until now, been confirmed by history. The broad experience of mankind allows us to postulate that it has no practical viability: it is not possible to harmonize the economic and political domination of a people, whatever may be the degree of their social development, with the preservation of their cultural personality.

In order to escape this choice—which may be called the *dilemma of cultural resistance*—imperialist colonial domination has tried to create theories which, in fact, are only gross formulations of racism, and which, in practice, are translated into a permanent state of siege of the indigenous populations on the basis of racist dictatorship (or democracy).

This, for example, is the case with the so-called theory of progressive *assimilation* of native populations, which turns out to be only a more or less violent attempt to deny the culture of the people in question. The utter failure of this "theory," implemented in practice by several colonial powers, including Portugal, is the most obvious proof of its lack of viability, if not of its inhuman character. It attains the highest degree of absurdity in the Portuguese case, where Salazar affirmed that Africa does *not exist.*

This is also the case with the so-called theory of apartheid, created, applied and developed on the basis of the economic and political domination of the people of Southern Africa by a racist minority, with all the outrageous crimes against humanity which that involves. The practice of apartheid takes the form of unrestrained exploitation of the labor force of the African masses, incarcerated and repressed in the largest concentration camp mankind has ever known.

These practical examples give a measure of the drama of foreign imperialist domination as it confronts the cultural reality of the dominated people. They also suggest the strong, dependent and reciprocal relationships existing between the *cultural situation* and the *economic* (and political) *situation* in the behavior of human societies. In fact, culture is always in the life of a society (open or closed), the more or less conscious result of the economic and political activities of that society, the more or less dynamic expression of the kinds of relationships which prevail in that society, on the one hand between man (considered individually or collectively) and nature, and, on the other hand, among individuals, groups of individuals, social strata or classes.

The value of culture as an element of resistance to foreign domination lies in the fact that culture is the vigorous manifestation on the ideological or idealist plane of the physical and historical reality of the society that is dominated or to be dominated. Culture is simultaneously the fruit of a people's history and a determinant of history, by the positive or negative influence which it exerts on the evolution of relationships between man and his environment, among men or groups of men within a society, as well as among different societies. Ignorance of this fact may explain the failure of several attempts at foreign domination—as well as the failure of some international liberation movements.

Let us examine the nature of *national liberation*. We shall consider this historical phenomenon in its contemporary context, that is, national liberation in opposition to imperialist domination. The latter is, as we know, distinct both in form and in content from preceding types of foreign domination (tribal, military-aristocratic, feudal, and capitalist domination in the free competition era).

The principal characteristic, common to every kind of imperialist domination, is the negation of the *historical process* of the dominated people by means of violently usurping the free operation of the process of development of the *productive*

41

forces. Now, in any given society, the level of development of the productive forces and the system for social utilization of these forces (the ownership system) determine the *mode of production.* In our opinion, the mode of production whose contradictions are manifested with more or less intensity through the class struggle, is the principal factor in the history of any human group, the level of the productive forces being the true and permanent driving power of history.

For every society, for every group of people, considered as an evolving entity, the level of the productive forces indicates the stage of development of the society and of each of its components in relation to nature, its capacity to act or to react consciously in relation to nature. It indicates and conditions the type of material relationships (expressed objectively or subjectively) which exists among the various elements or groups constituting the society in question. Relationships and types of relationships between man and nature, between man and his environment. Relationships and type of relationships among the individual or collective components of a society. To speak of these is to speak of history, but it is also to speak of culture.

Whatever may be the ideological or idealistic characteristics of cultural expression, culture is an essential element of the history of a people. Culture is, perhaps, the product of this history just as the flower is the product of a plant. Like history, or because it is history, culture has as its material base the level of the productive forces and the mode of production. Culture plunges its roots into the physical reality of the environmental humus in which it develops, and it reflects the organic nature of the society, which may be more or less influenced by external factors. History allows us to know the nature and extent of the imbalances and conflicts (economic, political and social) which characterize the evolution of a society; culture allows us to know the dynamic syntheses which have been developed and established by social conscience to resolve these conflicts at each stage of its evolution, in the search for survival and progress.

Just as happens with the flower in a plant, in culture there lies the capacity (or the responsibility) for forming and fertilizing the seedling which will assure the continuity of history, at the same time assuring the prospects for evolution and progress of the society in question. Thus it is understood that imperialist domination, by denying the historical development of the dominated people, necessarily also denies their cultural development. It is also understood why imperialist domination, like all other foreign domination, for its own security, requires cultural oppression and the attempt at direct or indirect liquidation of the essential elements of the culture of the dominated people.

The study of the history of national liberation struggles shows that generally these struggles are preceded by an increase in expression of culture, consolidated progressively into a successful or unsuccessful attempt to affirm the cultural personality of the dominated people, as a means of negating the oppressor culture. Whatever may be the conditions of a people's political and social factors in practicing this domination, it is generally within the culture that we find the seed of opposition, which leads to the structuring and development of the liberation movement.

In our opinion, the foundation for national liberation rests in the inalienable right of every people to have their own history, whatever formulations may be adopted at the level of international law. The objective of national liberation, is therefore, to reclaim the right, usurped by imperialist domination, namely: the liberation of the process of development of national productive forces. Therefore, national liberation takes place when, and only when, national productive forces are completely free of all kinds of foreign domination. The liberation of productive forces and consequently the ability to determine the mode of production most appropriate to the evolution of the liberated people, necessarily opens up new prospects for the cultural development of the society in question, by returning to that society all its capacity to create progress.

A people who free themselves from foreign domination will be free culturally only if, without complexes and without underestimating the importance of positive accretions from the oppressor and other cultures, they return to the upward paths of their own culture, which is nourished by the living reality of its environment, and which negates both harmful influences and any kind of subjection to foreign culture. Thus, it may be seen that if imperialist domination has the vital need to practice cultural oppression, national liberation is necessarily an act of *culture.*

On the basis of what has just been said, we may consider the national liberation movement as the organized political expression of the culture of the people who are undertaking the struggle. For this reason, those who lead the movement must have a clear idea of the value of the culture in the framework of the struggle and must have a thorough knowledge of the people's culture, whatever may be their level of economic development.

In our time it is common to affirm that all peoples have a culture. The time is past when, in an effort to perpetuate the domination of people, culture was considered an attribute of priviliged peoples or nations, and when, out of either ignorance or malice, culture was confused with technical power, if not with skin color of the shape of one's eyes. The liberation movement, as representative and defender of the culture of the people, must be conscious of the fact that, whatever may be the material conditions of the society it represents, the society is the bearer and creator of culture. The liberation movement must furthermore embody the mass character, the popular character of the culture —which is not and never could be the privilege of one or of some sectors of the society.

In the thorough analysis of social structure which every liberation movement should be capable of making in relation to the imperative of the struggle, the cultural characteristics of each group in society have a place of prime importance. For, while the culture has a mass character, it is not uniform, it is not equally developed in all sectors of society. The attitude of each social group toward the liberation struggle is dictated by its economic interests, but is also influenced profoundly by its culture. It may even be admitted that these differences in cultural levels explain differences in behavior toward the liberation movement on the part of individuals who belong to the same socio-economic group. It is at this point that culture reaches its full significance for each individual: understanding and integration into his environment, identification with fundamental problems and aspirations of the society, acceptance of the possibility of change in the direction of progress.

In the specific conditions of our country—and we would say, of Africa—the horizontal and vertical distribution of levels of culture is somewhat complex. In fact, from villages to towns, from one ethnic group to another, from one age group to another, from the peasant to the workman or to the indigenous intellectual who is more or less assimilated, and, as we have said, even from individual to individual within the same social group, the quantitative and qualitative level of culture varies significantly. It is of prime importance for the liberation movement to take these facts into consideration.

In societies with a horizontal social structure, such as the Balante, for example, the distribution of cultural levels is more or less uniform, variations being linked uniquely to characteristics of individuals or of age groups. On the other hand, in societies with a vertical structure, such as the Fula, there are important variations from the top to the bottom of the social pyramid. These differences in social structure illustrate once more the close relationship between culture and economy, and also explain differences in the general or sectoral behavior of these two ethnic groups in relation to the liberation movement.

It is true that the multiplicity of social and ethnic groups complicates the effort to determine the role of culture in the liberation movement. But it is vital not to lose sight of the decisive importance of the liberation struggle, even when class structure is to appear to be in embryonic stages of development.

The experience of colonial domination shows that, in the effort to perpetuate exploitation, the colonizers not only creates a system to repress the cultural life of the colonized people; he also provokes and develops the cultural alienation of a part of the population, either by so-called assimilation of indigenous people, or by creating a social gap between the indigenous elites and the popular masses. As a result of this process of dividing or of deepening the divisions in the society, it happens that a considerable part of the population, notably the urban or peasant *petite bourgeoisie,* assimilates the colonizer's mentality, considers itself culturally superior to its own people and ignores or looks down upon their cultural values. This situation, characteristic of the majority of colonized intellectuals, is consolidated by increases in the social privileges of the assimilated or alienated group with direct implications for the behavior of individuals in this group in relation to the liberation movement. A reconversion of minds—of mental set—is thus indispensable to the true integration of people into the liberation movement. Such reconversion—re-Africanization, in our case—may take place before the struggle, but it is completed only during the course of the struggle, through daily contact with the popular masses in the communion of sacrifice required by the struggle.

However, we must take into account the fact that, faced with with the prospect of political independence, the ambition and opportunism from which the liberation movement generally suffers may bring into the struggle unconverted individuals. The latter, on the basis of their level of schooling, their scientific or technical knowledge, but without losing any of their social class biases, may attain the highest positions in the liberation movement. Vigilance is thus indispensable on the cultural as well as the political plane. For, in the liberation movement as elsewhere, all that glitters is not necessarily gold: political leaders—even the most famous—may be culturally alienated people. But the social class characteristics of the culture are even more discernible in the behavior of privileged groups in rural areas, especially in the case of ethnic groups with a vertical social structure, where, nevertheless, assimilation or cultural alienation influences are non-existent or practically non-existent. This is the case, for example, with the Fula ruling class. Under colonial domination, the political authority of this class (traditional chiefs, noble families, religious leaders) is purely nominal, and the popular masses know that true authority lies with and is acted upon by colonial administrators. However, the ruling class preserves in essence its basic cultural authority over the masses and this has very important political implications.

Recognizing this reality, the colonizer who represses or inhibits significant cultural activity on the part of the masses at the base of the social pyramid, strengthens and protects the prestige and the cultural influence of the ruling class at the summit. The colonizer installs chiefs who support him and who are to some degree accepted by the masses; he gives these chiefs material privileges such as education for their eldest children, creates chiefdoms where they did not exist before, develops cordial relations with religious leaders, builds mosques, organizes journeys to Mecca, etc. And above all, by means of the repressive organs of colonial administration, he guarantees economic and social privileges to the ruling class in their relations with the masses. All this does not make it impossible that, among these ruling classes, there may be individuals or groups of individuals who join the liberation movement, although less frequently than in the case of the assimilated "petite bourgeoisie." Several traditional and religious leaders join the struggle at the very beginning or during its development, making an enthusiastic contribution to the cause of liberation.

But here again vigilance is indispensable: preserving deep down the cultural prejudices of their class, individuals in this category generally see in the liberation movement the only valid means, using the sacrifices of the masses, to eliminate colonial oppression of their own class and to re-establish in this way their complete political and cultural domination of the people.

✸In the general framework of contesting colonial imperialist domination and in the actual situation to which we refer, among the oppressor's most loyal allies are found some high officials and intellectuals of the liberal professions, assimilated people, and also a significant number of representatives of the ruling class from rural areas. This fact gives some measure of the influence (positive or negative) of culture and cultural prejudices in the problem of political choice when one is confronted with the liberation movement. It also illustrates the limits of this influence and the supremacy of the class factor in the behavior of the different social groups. The high official or the assimilated intellectual, characterized by total cultural alienation, identifies himself by political choice with the traditional or religious leader who has experienced no significant foreign cultural influences.

For these two categories of people place above all principles or demands of a cultural nature—and against the aspirations of the people—their own economic and social privileges, their own *class interests*. That is a truth which the liberation movement cannot afford to ignore without risking betrayal of the economic, political, social and cultural objectives of the struggle. ✸

Without minimizing the positive contribution which privileged classes may bring to the struggle, the liberation movement must, on the cultural level just as on the political level, base its action in popular culture, whatever may be the diversity of levels of cultures in the country. The cultural combat against colonial domination—the first phase of the liberation movement —can be planned efficiently only on the basis of the culture of the rural and urban working masses, including the nationalist (revolutionary) "petite bourgeoisie" who have been re-Africanized or who are ready for cultural reconversion. Whatever may be the complexity of this basic cultural panorama, the liberation movement must be capable of distinguishing within it the essential from the secondary, the postive from the negative, the progressive from the reactionary in order to characterize the master line which defines progressively a *national culture*.

In order for culture to play the important role which falls to it in the framework of the liberation movement, the movement must be able to preserve the positive cultural values of every well-defined social group, of every category, and to achieve the confluence of these values in the service of the struggle, giving it a new dimension—the *national dimension*. Confronted with such a necessity, the liberation struggle is, above all, a struggle both for the preservation and survival of the cultural values of the people and for the harmonization and development of these values within a national framework.

The political and moral unity of the liberation movement and of the people it represents and directs implies achieving the cultural unity of the social groups which are of key importance for the liberation struggle. This unity is achieved on the one hand by total identification with the environmental reality and with the fundamental problems and aspirations of the people; and, on the other hand, by progressive cultural identification of the various social groups participating in the struggle.

As it progresses the liberation struggle must bring diverse interests into harmony, resolve contradictions and define common objectives in the search for liberty and progress. The taking to heart of its objectives by large strata in the population, reflected in their determination in the face of difficulties and sacrifices, is a great political and moral victory. It is also a cultural achievement of decisive importance for the subsequent development and success of the liberation movement.

The greater the differences between the culture of the dominated people and the culture of their oppressor, the more possible such a victory becomes. History proves that it is much less difficult to dominate and to continue dominating a people whose culture is similar or analogous to that of the conqueror. It could be contended that the failure of Napoleon, whatever may have been the economic and political motivations of his wars of conquest, resulted from his ignorance of this principle, or from his inability to limit his ambition to the domination of peoples whose culture was more or less similar to that of France. The same thing could be said about other ancient, modern, or contemporary empires.

One of the most serious errors, if not the most serious error, committed by colonial powers in Africa, may have been to ignore or underestimate the cultural strength of African peoples. This attitude is particularly clear in the case of Portuguese colonial domination, which has not been content with denying absolutely the existence of the cultural values of the African and his social position but has persisted in forbidding him all kinds of political activity. The people of Portugal, who have not even enjoyed the wealth taken from African peoples by Portuguese colonialism, but the majority of whom have assimilated the imperial mentality of the country's ruling classes, are paying very dearly today, in three colonial wars, for the mistake of underestimating our cultural reality.

The political and armed resistance of the people of the Portuguese colonies, as of other countries or regions of Africa, was crushed by the technical superiority of the imperialist conqueror, with the complicity of or betrayal by some indigenous ruling classes. Those elites who were loyal to the history and to the culture of the people were destroyed. Entire populations were massacred. The colonial kingdom was established with all the crimes and exploitation which characterize it. But cultural resistance of the African people was not destroyed. Repressed persecuted, betrayed by some social groups who were in league with the colonialists, African culture survived all the storms, taking refuge in the villages, in the forests and in the spirit of the generations who were victims of colonialism. Like the seed which long awaits conditions favorable to germination in order to assure the survival of the species and its development, the culture of African peoples flourishes again today, across the continent, in struggles for national liberation. Whatever may be the forms of these struggles, their successes or failures, and the length of their development, they mark the beginning of a new era in the history of the continent and are both in form and in content the most important cultural element in the life of African peoples. The freedom struggle of African peoples is both the fruit and the proof of cultural vigor, opening up new prospects for the development of culture in the service of progress.

The time is past when it was necessary to seek arguments to prove the cultural maturity of African peoples. The irrationality of the racist "theories" of a Gobineau or a Levy-Bruhl neither

49

interests nor convinces anyone but racists. In spite of colonial domination (and perhaps even because of this domination), Africa was able to impose respect for her cultural values. She even showed herself to be one of the richest of continents in cultural values. From Carthage to Giza to Zimbabwe, from Meroe to Benin and Ife, from Sahara or Timbuktu to Kilwa, across the immensity and the diversity of the continent's natural conditions, the culture of African peoples is an undeniable reality: in works of art as well as in oral and written traditions, in cosmological conceptions as well as in music and dance, in religions and belief as well as in the dynamic balance of economic political and social structures created by African man.

The universal value of African culture is now an incontestable fact; nevertheless, it should not be forgotten that African man, whose hands, as the poet said, "placed the stones of the foundations of the world," has developed his culture frequently, if not constantly, in adverse conditions: from deserts to equatorial forests, from coastal marshes to the banks of great rivers subject to frequent flooding, in spite of all sorts of difficulties, including plagues which have destroyed plants and animals and man alike. In agreement with Basil Davidson and other researchers in African history and culture, we can say that the accomplishments of the African genius in economic, political, social and cultural domains, despite the inhospitable character of the environment, are epic—comparable to the major historical examples of the greatness of man.

Of course, this reality constitutes a reason for pride and a stimulus to those who fight for the liberation and the progress of African peoples. But it is important not to lose sight of the fact that no culture is a perfect, finished whole. Culture, like history, is an expanding and developing phenomenon. Even more important, we must take account of the fact that the fundamental characteristic of a culture is the highly dependent and reciprocal nature of its linkages with the social and economic reality of the environment, with the level of productive forces and the mode of production of the society which created it.

Culture, the fruit of history, reflects at every moment the material and spiritual reality of society, of man-the-individual and of man-the-social-being, faced with conflicts which set him against nature and the exigencies of common life. From this we see that all culture is composed of essential and secondary elements, of strengths and weaknesses, of virtues and failings, of positive and negative aspects, of factors of progress and factors of stagnation or regression. From this also we can see that culture—the creation of society and the synthesis of the balances and the solutions which society engenders to resolve the conflicts which characterize each phase of its history—is a social reality, independent of the will of men, the color of their skins or the shape of their eyes.

A thorough analysis of cultural reality does not permit the claim that there exist continental or racial cultures. This is because, as with history, the development of culture proceeds in uneven fashion, whether at the level of a continent, a "race," or even a society. The coordinates of culture, like those of any developing phenomenon, vary in space and time, whether they be material (physical) or human (biological and social). The fact of recognizing the existence of common and particular features in the cultures of African peoples, independent of the color of their skin, does not necessarily imply that one and only one culture exists on the continent. In the same way that from a economic and political viewpoint we can recognize the existence of several Africas, so also there are many African cultures.

Without any doubt, underestimation of the cultural values of African peoples, based upon racist feelings and upon the intention of perpetuating foreign exploitation of Africans, has done much harm to Africa. But in the face of the vital need for progress, the following attitudes or behaviors will be no less harmful to Africa: indiscriminate compliments; systematic exaltation of virtues without condemning faults; blind acceptance of the values of the culture, without considering what presently or potentially regressive elements it contains; confusion between what is the expression of an objective and material historical reality and what appears to be a creation of the mind or the product of a peculiar temperament; absurd linking of artistic creations, whether good or not, with supposed racial characteristics; and finally, the non-scientific or a scientific critical appreciation of the cultural phenomenon.

Thus, the important thing is not to lose time in more or less idle discussion of the specific or unspecific characteristics of African cultural values, but rather to look upon these values as a conquest of a small piece of humanity for the common heritage of humanity, achieved in one or several phases of its evolution.

RETURN TO THE SOURCE

The important thing is to proceed to critical analysis of African cultures in relation to the liberation movement and to the exigencies of progress—confronting this new stage in African history. It is important to be conscious of the value of African cultures in the framework of universal civilization, but to compare this value with that of other cultures, not with a view of deciding its superiority or inferiority, but in order to determine, in the general framework of the struggle for progress, what contribution African culture has made and can make, and what are the contributions it can or must receive from elsewhere.

The liberation movement must, as we have said, base its action upon thorough knowledge of the culture of the people and be able to appreciate at their true value the elements of this culture, as well as the different levels that it reaches in each social group. The movement must also be able to discern in the entire set of cultural values of the people the essential and the secondary, the positive and the negative, the progressive and the reactionary, the strengths and the weaknesses. All this is necessary as a function of the demands of the struggle and in order to be able to concentrate action on what is essential without forgetting what is secondary, to induce development of positive and progressive elements, and to combat with flexibility but with rigor the negative and reactionary elements; and finally, in order to utilize strengths efficiently and to eliminate weaknesses or to transform them into strengths.

The more one realizes that the chief goal of the liberation movement goes beyond the achievement of political independence to the superior level of complete liberation of the productive forces and the construction of economic, social and cultural progress of the people, the more evident is the necessity of undertaking a selective analysis of the values of the culture within the framework of the struggle for liberation. The need for such an analysis of cultural values becomes more acute when, in order to face colonial violence, the liberation movement must mobilize and organize the people, under the direction of a strong and disciplined political organization, in order to resort to violence in the cause of freedom—*the armed struggle for the national liberation.*

Generally, the negative values of culture are generally an obstacle to the development of the struggle and to the building of this progress. In this perspective, the liberation movement must be able, beyond the analysis mentioned above, to achieve gradually but surely as its political action develops the *confluence of the levels* of culture of the different social groups available for the struggle. The movement must be able to transform them into the national cultural force which undergirds and conditions the development of the armed struggle. It should be noted that the analysis of cultural reality already gives a measure of the strengths and weaknesses of the people when confronted with the demands of the struggle, and therefore represents a valuable contribution to the strategy and tactics to be followed, on the political as well as on the military plane. But only during the struggle, launched from a satisfactory base of political and moral unity, is the complexity of cultural problems raised in all its dimensions. This frequently requires successive adaptations of strategy and tactics to the realities which only the struggle is capable of revealing. Experience of the struggle shows how utopian and absurd it is to profess to apply without considering local reality (and especially cultural reality) plans of action developed by other peoples during their liberation struggles and to apply solutions which they found to the problems with which they were or are confronted.

It can be said that at the outset of the struggle, whatever may have been the extent of preparation undertaken, both the leadership of the liberation movement and the militant and popular masses have no clear awareness of the strong influence of cultural values in the development of the struggle, the possibilities culture creates, the limits it imposes, and above all, how; and how much culture is for the people an inexhaustible source of courage, of material and moral support, of physical and psychic energy which enables them to accept sacrifices— even to accomplish "miracles." But equally, in some respects, culture is very much a source of obstacles and difficulties, of erroneous conceptions about reality, of deviation in carrying out duty, and of limitations on the tempo and efficiency of a struggle that is confronted with the political, technical and scientific requirements of a war.

The armed struggle for liberation, launched in response to the colonialist oppressor, turns out to be a painful but efficient instrument for developing the cultural level of both the leadership strata in the liberation movement and the various social groups who participate in the struggle.

RETURN TO THE SOURCE

The leaders of the liberation movement, drawn generally from the "petite bourgeoisie" (intellectuals, clerks) or the urban working class (workers, chauffeurs, salary-earners in general), having to live day by day with the various peasant groups in the heart of the rural populations, come to know the people better. They discover at the grass roots the richness of their cultural values (philosophic, political, artistic, social and moral), acquire a clearer understanding of the economic realities of the country, of the problems, sufferings and hopes of the popular masses. The leaders realize, not without a certain astonishment, the richness of spirit, the capacity for reasoned discussion and clear exposition of ideas, the facility for understanding and assimilating concepts on the part of populations groups who yesterday were forgotten, if not despised, and who were considered incompetent by the colonizer and even by some nationals. The leaders thus enrich their cultures—develop personally their capacity to serve the movement in the service of the people.

On their side, the working masses and, in particular, the peasants who are usually illiterate and never have moved beyond the boundaries of their village or region, in contact with other groups lose the complexes which constrained them in their relationships with other ethnic and social groups. They realize their crucial role in the struggle; they break the bonds of the village universe to integrate progressively into the country and the world; they acquire an infinite amount of new knowledge, useful for their immediate and future activity within the framework of the struggle, and they strengthen their political awareness by assimilating the principles of national and social revolution postulated by the struggle. They thereby become more able to play the decisive role of providing the principal force behind the liberation movement.

As we know, the armed liberation struggle requires the mobilization and organization of a significant majority of the population, the political and moral unity of the various social classes, the efficient use of modern arms and of other means of war, the progressive liquidation of the remnants of tribal mentality, and the rejection of social and religious rules and taboos which inhibit development of the struggle (gerontocracies, nepotism, social inferiority of women, rites and practices which are incompatible with the rational and national character of the struggle, etc.). The struggle brings about other profound modifications in the life of populations. The armed liberation struggle implies, therefore, a veritable forced march along the road to cultural progress.

Consider these features inherent in an armed liberation struggle: the practice of democracy, of criticism and self-criticism, the increasing responsibility of populations for the direction of their lives, literacy work, creation of schools and health services, training of cadres from peasant and worker backgrounds—and many other achievements. When we consider these features, we see that the armed liberation struggle is not only a product of culture but also a *determinant of culture*. This is without doubt for the people the prime recompense for the efforts and sacrifices which war demands. In this perspective, it behooves the liberation movement to define clearly the objectives of cultural resistance as an integral and determining part of the struggle.

From all that has just been said, it can be concluded that in the framework of the conquest of national independence and in the perspective of developing the economic and social progress of the people, the objectives must be at least the following: *development of a popular culture* and of all positive indigenous cultural values; *development of a national* cuture based upon the history and the achievements of the struggle itself; constant promotion of the *political and moral awareness* of the people (of all social groups) as well as *patriotism*, of the spirit of sacrifice and devotion to the cause of independence, of justice, and of progress; development of a technical, technological, and *scientific culture*, compatible with the requirements for progress; development, on the basis of a critical assimilation of man's achievements in the domains of art, science, literature, etc., of a *universal culture* for perfect integration into the contemporary world, in the perspectives of its evolution; constant and generalized promotion of feelings of humanism, of solidarity, of respect and disinterested devotion to human beings.

The achievement of these objectives is indeed possible, because the armed struggle for liberation, in the concrete conditions of life of African peoples, confronted with the imperialist challenge, is an act of insemination upon history—the major expression of our culture and of our African essence. In the moment of victory, it must be translated into a significant leap forward of the culture of the people who are liberating themselves.

If that does not happen, then the efforts and sacrifices accepted during the struggle will have been made in vain. The struggle will have failed to achieve its objectives, and the people will have missed an opportunity for progress in the general framework of history.

Identity and Dignity in the Context of the National Liberation Struggle

On October 15, 1972 Amilcar Cabral received an hono-rary doctorate degree at Lincoln University, Pennsylvania. This was his address on that occasion.

INTRODUCTION

The people's struggle for national liberation and independ-ence from imperialist rule has become a driving force of prog-ress for humanity and undoubtedly constitutes one of the essential characteristics of contemporary history.

An objectve analysis of imperialism insofar as it is a fact or a "natural" historical phenomenon, indeed "necessary" in the con-text of the type of economic political evolution of an important part of humanity, reveals that imperialist rule, with all its train of wretchedness, of pillage, of crime and of destruction of human and cultural values, was not just a negative reality. The vast accumulation of capital in half a dozen countries of the northern hemisphere which was the result of piracy, of the confiscation of the property of other peoples and of the ruthless exploitation of the work of these peoples will not only lead to the monopolization of colonies, but to the division of the world, and more imperialist rule.

RETURN TO THE SOURCE

In the rich countries imperialist capital, constantly seeking to enlarge itself, increased the creative capacity of man and brought about a total transformation of the means of production thanks to the rapid progress of science, of techniques and of technology. This accentuated the pooling of labor and brought about the ascension of huge areas of population. In the colonized countries where colonization on the whole blocked the historical process of the development of the subjected peoples or else eliminated them radically or progressively, imperialist capital imposed new types of relationships on indigenous society, the structure of which became more complex and it stirred up, fomented, poisoned or resolved contradictions and social conflicts; it introduced together with money and the development of internal and external markets, new elements in the economy, it brought about the birth of new nations from human groups or from peoples who were at different stages of historical development.

It is not to defend imperialist domination to recognize that it gave new nations to the world, the dimensions of which it reduced and that it revealed new stages of development in human societies and in spite of or because of the prejudices, the discrimination and the crimes which it occasioned, it contributed to a deeper knowledge of humanity as a moving whole, as a unity in the complex diversity of the characteristics of its development.

Imperialist rule on many continents favored a multilateral and progressive (sometimes abrupt) confirmation not only between different men but also between different societies. The practice of imperialist rule—its affirmation or its negation—demanded (and still demands) a more or less accurate knowledge of the society it rules and of the historical reality (both economic, social, and cultural) in the middle of which it exists. This knowledge is necessarily exposed in terms of comparison with the dominating subject and with its own historical reality. Such a knowledge is a vital necessity in the practice of imperialist rule which results in the confrontation, mostly violent, between two identities which are totally dissimilar in their historical elements and contradictory in their different functions. The search for such a knowledge contributed to a general enrichment of human and social knowledge in spite of the fact that it was one-sided, subjective, and very often unjust.

In fact, man has never shown as much interest in knowing other men and other societies as during this century of imperialist domination. An unprecedented mass of information, of hypotheses and theories has been built up, notably in the fields of history, ethnology, ethnography, sociology, and culture concerning people or groups brought under imperialist domination. The concepts of race, caste, ethnicity, tribe, nation, culture, identity, dignity, and many others, have become the object of increasing attention from those who study men and the societies described as "primitive" or "evolving."

More recently, with the rise of liberation movements, the need has arisen to analyze the character of these societies in the light of the struggle they are waging, and to decide the factors which launch or hold back this struggle. The researchers are generally agreed that in this context culture shows special significance. So one can argue that any attempt to clarify the true role of culture in the development of the (pre-independence) liberation movement can make a useful contribution to the broad struggle of the people against imperialist domination.

In this short lecture, we consider particularly the problems of the "return to the source," and of identity and dignity in the context of the national liberation movement.

PART I

The fact that independence movements are generally marked, even in their early stages, by an upsurge of cultural activity, has led to the view that such movements are preceded by a "cultural renaissance" of the subject people. Some go as far as to suggest that culture is one means of collecting together a group, even a *weapon* in the struggle for independence.

From the experience of our own struggle and one might say that of the whole of Africa, we consider that there is too limited, even a mistaken idea of the vital role of culture in the development of the liberation movement. In our view, this arises from a fake generalization of a phenomenon which is real but limited which is at a particular level in the vertical structure of colonized societies—at the level of the *elite* or the colonial *diasporas*. This generalization is unaware of or ignores the vital element of the problem: the indestructible character of the cultural resistance of the masses of the people when confronted with foreign domination.

Certainly imperialist domination calls for cultural oppression and attempts either directly or indirectly to do away with the most important elements of the culture of the subject people. But the people are only able to create and develop the liberation movement because they keep their culture alive despite continual and organized repression of their cultural life and because they continue to resist culturally even when their politico-military resistance is destroyed. And it is cultural resistance which, at a given moment, can take on new forms, i.e., political, economic, armed to fight foreign domination.

With certain exceptions, *the period of colonization* was not long enough, at least in Africa, for there to be a significant degree of destruction or damage of the most important facets of the culture and traditions of the subject people. Colonial experience of imperialist domination in Africa (genocide, racial segregation and apartheid excepted) shows that the only so-called positive solution which the colonial power put forward to repudiate the subject people's cultural resistance was *"assimilation."* But the complete failure of the policy of "progressive assimilation" of native populations is the living proof both of the falsehood of this theory and of the capacity of the subject people to resist. As far as the Portuguese colonies are concerned, the maximum number of people assimilated was 0.3% of the total population (in Guine) and this was after 500 years of civilizing influence and half a century of "colonial peace."

On the other hand, even in the settlements where the overwhelming majority of the population are indigenous peoples, the area occupied by the colonial power and especially the area of *cultural influence* is usually restricted to coastal strips and to a few limited parts in the interior. Outside the boundaries of the capital and other urban centers, the influence of the colonial power's culture is almost nil. It only leaves its mark at the very top of the colonial social pyramid—which created colonialism itself—and particularly it influences what one might call the "indigenous lower middle class" and a very small number of workers in urban areas.

It can thus be seen that the masses in the rural areas, like a large section of the urban population, say, in all, over 99% of the indigenous population are untouched or almost untouched by the culture of the colonial power. This situation is partly the result of the necessarily obscurantist character of the imperialist domination which while it despises and suppresses indigenous culture takes no interest in promoting culture for the masses who are their pool for forced labor and the main object of exploitation. It is also the result of the effectiveness of cultural resistance of the people, who when they are subjected to political domination and economic exploitation find that their own culture acts as a bulwark in preserving their *identity*. Where the indigenous society has a vertical structure, this defense of their cultural heritage is further strengthened by the colonial power's interest in protecting and backing the cultural influence of the ruling classes, their allies.

The above argument implies that generally speaking there is not any marked destruction or damage to culture or tradition, neither for the masses in the subject country nor for the indigenous ruling classes (traditional chief, noble families, religious authorities). Repressed, persecuted, humiliated, betrayed by certain social groups who have compromised with the foreign power, culture took refuge in the villages, in the forests, and in the spirit of the victims of domination. Culture survives all these challenges and through the struggle for liberation blossoms forth again. Thus the question of a "return to the source" or of a "cultural renaissance" does not arise and could not arise for the masses of these people, for it is they who are the repository of the culture and at the same time the only social sector who can preserve and build it up and *make history*.

Thus, in Africa at least, for a true idea of the real role which culture plays in the development of the liberation movement a distinction must be made between the situation of the masses, who preserve their culture, and that of the social groups who are assimilated or partially so, who are cut off and culturally alienated, Even though the indigenous colonial elite who emerged during the process of colonization still continue to pass on some element of indigenous culture yet they live both materially and spiritually according to the foreign colonial culture. They seek to identify themselves increasingly with this culture both in their social behaviors and even in their appreciation of its values.

In the course of two or three generations of colonization, a social class arises made up of civil servants, people who are employed in various branches of the economy, especially commerce, professional people, and a few urban and agricultural landowners. This indigenous petite bourgeosie which emerged out of foreign domination and is indispensable to the system of colonial exploitation, stands midway between the masses of the working class in town and country and the small number of local representatives of the foreign ruling class. Although they may have quite strong links with the masses and with the traditional chiefs, generally speaking, they aspire to a way of life which is similar if not identical with that of the foreign minority. At the same time while they restrict their dealings with the masses, they try to become integrated into this minority often at the cost of family or ethnic ties and always at great personal cost. Yet despite the apparent exceptions, they do not succeed in getting past the barriers thrown up by the system. They are prisoners of the cultural and social contradictions of their lives. They cannot escape from their role as a marginal class, or a "marginalized" class.

The marginal character or the "marginality" of this class both in their own country and in the *diasporas established in the territory* of the colonial power is responsible for the socio-cultural conflicts of the colonial elite or the indigenous petite bourgeoisie, played out very much according to their material circumstances and level of acculturation but always at the individual level, never collectively.

It is within the framework of this daily drama, against the backcloth of the usually violent confrontation between the mass of the people and the ruling colonial class that a feeling of bitterness or a *frustration complex* is bred and develops among the indigenous petite bourgeoisie. At the same time, they are becoming more and more conscious of a compelling need to question their marginal status, and to re-discover an identity.

Thus, they turn to the people around them, the people at the other extreme of the socio-cultural conflict—the native masses. For this reason arises the problem of "return to the source" which seems to be even more pressing the greater is the isolation of the petite bourgeoisie (or native elites) and their acute feelings of frustration as in the case of African diasporas living in the colonial or racist metropolis. It comes as no surprise that the theories or "movements" such as *Pan-Africanism* or *Negritude* (two pertinent expressions arising mainly from the assumption that all black Africans have a cultural identity) were propounded outside black Africa. More recently, the Black Americans' claim to an African identity is another proof, possibly rather a desperate one, of the need for a "return to the source" although clearly it is influenced by a new situation: the fact that the great majority of African people are now independent.

But the "return to the source" is not and cannot in itself be an *act of struggle* against foreign domination (colonialist and racist) and it no longer necessarily means a return to traditions. It is the denial, by the petite bourgeoisie, of the pretended supremacy of the culture of the dominant power over that of the dominated people with which it must identify itself. The "return to the source" is therefore not a voluntary step, but the only possible reply to the demand of concrete need, historically determined, and enforced by the inescapable contradiction between the colonized society and the colonial power, the mass of the people exploited and the foreign exploitive class, a contradiction in the light of which each social stratum or indigenous class must define its position.

When the "return to the source" goes beyond the individual and is expressed through "groups" or "movements," the contradiction is transformed into struggle (secret or overt), and is a prelude to the pre-independence movement or of the struggle for liberation from the foreign yoke. So, the "return to the source" is of no historical importance unless it brings not only real involvement in the struggle for independence, but also complete and absolute identification with the hopes of the mass of the people, who contest not only the foreign culture but also the foreign domination as a whole. Otherwise, the "return to the source" is nothing more than an attempt to find short-term benefits—knowingly or unknowingly a kind of polical opportunism.

One must point out that the "return to the source," apparent or real, does not develop at one time and in the same way in the heart of the indigenous petite bourgeoisie. It is a slow process, broken up and uneven, whose development depends on the degree of acculturation of each individual, of the material circumstances of his life, on the forming of his ideas and on his experience as a social being. This uneveness is the basis of the split of the indigenous petite bourgeoisie into three groups when confronted with the liberation movement: a) a minority, which, even if it wants to see an end to foreign domination,

63

clings to the dominant colonialist class and openly oppose the movement to protect its social position; b) a majority of people who are hesitant and indecisive; c) another minority of people who share in the building and leadership of the liberation movement.

But the latter group, which plays a decisive role in the development of the pre-independence movement, does not truly identify with the mass of the people (with their culture and hopes) except through struggle, the scale of this identification depending on the kind or methods of struggle, on the ideological basis of the movement and on the level of moral and political awareness of each individual.

PART II

Identification of a section of the indigenous *petite bourgeoisie* with the mass of the people has an essential prerequisite: *that, in the face of destructive action by imperialist domination, the masses retain their identity,* separate and distinct from that of the colonial power. It is worthwhile therefore to decide in what circumstances this retention is possible; why, when and at what levels of the dominated society is raised the problem of the loss or absence of identity: and in consequence it becomes necessary to assert or reassert in the framework of the pre-independence movement a separate and distinct identity from that of the colonial power.

The identity of an individual or a particular group of people is a bio-sociological factor outside the will of that individual or group, but which is meaningful only when it is expressed in relation to other individuals or other groups. The dialectical character of identity lies in the fact that an individual (or a group) is only similar to certain individuals (or groups) if it is also different to other individuals (or groups).

The definition of an identity, individual or collective, is at the same time the affirmation and denial of a certain number of characteristics which define the individuals or groups, through *historical* (biological and sociological) factors at a moment of their development. In fact, identity is not a constant, precisely because the biological and sociological factors which define it are in constant change. Biologically and sociologically, there are no two beings (individual or collective) completely the same or completely different, for it is always possible to find in them common or distinguishing characteristics. Therefore the identity of a being is always a relative quality, even circumstantial for defining it demands a selection, more or less rigid and strict, of the biological and sociological characteristics of the being in question. One must point out that in the fundamental binomial in the definition of identity, the sociological factors are more determining than the biological. In fact, if it is correct that the biological element (inherited genetic patrimony) is the inescapable physical basis of the existence and continuing growth of identity, it is no less correct that the sociological element is the factor which gives it objective substance by giving content and form, and allowing confrontation and comparison between individuals and between groups. To make a total definition of identity, the inclusion of the biological element is indispensable, but does not imply a sociological similarity, whereas two beings who are sociologically exactly the same must necessarily have similar biological identities.

This shows on the one hand the supremacy of the social over the individual condition, for society (human for example) is a higher form of life. It shows on the other hand the need not to confuse, the *original identity*, of which the biological element is the main determinant, and the *actual identity*, of which the main determinant is the sociological element. Clearly, the identity of which one must take account at a given moment of the growth of a being (individual or collective) is the actual identity, and awareness of that being reached only on the basis of his original identity is incomplete, partial and false, for it leaves out or does not comprehend the decisive influence of social conditions on the content and form of identity.

In the formation and development of individual or collective identity, the social condition is an objective agent, arising from economic, political, social and cultural aspects which are characteristic of the growth and history of the society in question. If one argues that the economic aspect is fundamental, one can assert that identity is in a certain sense the expression of an economic reality. This reality, whatever the geographical context and the path of development of the society, is defined by the level of productive forces (the relationship between man and nature) and by the means of production (the relations between men and between classes within this society). But if one accepts that culture is a dynamic synthesis of the material and spiritual conditon of the society and expresses relationship both between man and nature and between the different classes within a society, one can assert that identity is at the individual and collective level and beyond the economic condition, the expression of culture. This is why to attribute, recognize or declare the identity of an individual or group is above all to place that individual or group in the framework of a culture. Now as we all know, the main prop of culture in any society is the social structure. One can therefore draw the conclusion that the possibility of a movement group keeping (or losing) its identity in the face of foreign domination depends on the extent of the destruction of its social structure under the stresses of that domination.

As for the effects of imperialist domination on the social structure of the dominated people, one must look here at the case of classic colonialism against which the pre-independence movement is contending. In that case, whatever the stage of historical development of the dominated society, the social structure can be subjected to the following experiences: a) *total destruction,* mixed with immediate or gradual liquidation of the indigenous people and replacement by a foreign people; b) *partial destruction,* with the settling of a more or less numerous foreign population; c) *ostensible preservation,* brought about by the restriction of the indigenous people in geographical areas or special reserves usually without means of living, and the massive influx of a foreign population.

The fundamentally horizontal character of the social structure of African people, due to the profusion of ethnic groups, means that the cultural resistance and degree of retention of identity are not uniform. So, even where ethnic groups have broadly succeeded in keeping their identity, we observe that the most *resistant* groups are those which have had the most violent battles with the colonial power during the period of effective occupation* or those who because of their geographical location have had least contact with the foreign presence.**

One must point out that the attitude of the colonial power towards the ethnic groups creates an insoluble contradiction:

---

* In our country: Mandjaques, Pepels, Oincas, Balantes, Beafadas.
** Pajadincas and other minorities in the interior.

on the one hand it must divide or keep divisions in order to rule and for that reason favors separation if not conflict between ethnic groups; on the other hand to try to keep the permanency of its domination it needs to destroy the social structure, culture, and by implication identity, of these groups. Moreover, it must protect the ruling class of those groups which (like for example the Fula tribe or nation in our country) have given decisive support during the colonial conquest— a policy which favors the preservation of the identity of these groups.

As has already been said, there are not usually important changes in respect of culture in the upright shape of the indigenous social pyramids (groups or societies with a State). Each level or class keeps its identity, linked with that of the group but separate from that of other social classes. Conversely, in the urban centers as in some of the interior regions of the country where the cultural influence of the colonial power is felt, the problem of identity is more complicated. While the bottom and the top of the social pyramid (that is the mass of the working class drawn from different ethnic groups and the foreign dominant class) keep their identities, the middle level of this pyramid (the indigenous petite bourgeoise), culturally uprooted, alienated or more or less assimilated, engages in a sociological battle in search of its identity. One must also point out that though united by a new identity—granted by the colonial power—the foreign dominant class can not free itself from the contradictions of its own society, which it brings to the colonized country.

When, at the initiative of a minority of the indigenous petite bourgeoisie, allied with the indigenous masses, the pre-independence movement is launched, the masses have no need to assert or reassert their identity, which they have never confused nor would have known how to confuse with that of the colonial power. This need is felt only by the indigenous petite bourgeoisie which finds itself obliged to take up a position in the struggle which opposes the masses to the colonial power. However, the reassertion of identity distinct from that of the colonial power is not always achieved by all the petite bourgeoisie. It is only a minority who do this, while another minority asserts, often in a noisy manner, the identity of the foreign dominant class, while the silent majority is trapped in indecision.

Moreover, even when there is a reassertion of an identity distinct from that of the colonial power, therefore the same as that of the masses, it does not show itself in the same way everywhere. One part of the middle class minority engaged in the pre-independence movement, uses the foreign cultural norms, calling on literature and art, to express the discovery of its identity rather than to express the hopes and sufferings of the masses. And precisely because he uses the language and speech of the minority colonial power, he only occasionally manages to influence the masses, generally illiterate and familar with other forms of artistic expression. This does not however remove the value of the contribution of the development of the struggle made by this petite bourgeoise minority, for it can at the same time influence a sector of the uprooted or those who are late-comers to its own class and an important sector of public opinion in the colonial metropolis, notably the class of intellectuals.

The other part of the lower middle class which from the start joins in the pre-independence movement finds in its prompt share in the liberation struggle and in integration with the masses of the best means of expression of identity distinct from that of the colonial power.

That is why identification with the masses and reassertion of identity can be temporary or definitive, apparent or real, in the light of the daily efforts and sacrifices demanded by the struggle itself. A struggle, which while being the organized political expression of a *culture* is also and necessarily a proof not only of *identity* but also of *dignity*.

In the course of the process of colonialist domination, the masses, whatever the characteristic of the social structure of the group to which they belong, do not stop resisting the colonial power. In a first phase—that of conquest, cynically called "pacification"—they resist, gun in hand, foreign occupation. In a second phase—that of the golden age of triumphant colonial-ism—they offer the foreign domination passive resistance, almost silent, but blazoned with many revolts, usually individual and once in a while collective. The revolt is particularly in the field of work and taxes, even in social contacts with the repre-sentatives, foreign or indigenous of the colonial power. In a third phase—that of the liberation struggle—it is the masses who provide the main strength which employs political or armed resistance to challenge and to destroy foreign domination. Such a prolonged and varied resistance is possible only because while keeping their culture and identity, the masses keep intact the sense of their individual and collective dignity, despite the worries, humiliations and brutalities to which they are often subjected.

The assertion or reassertion by the indigenous petite bourgeoisie of identity distinct from that of the colonial power does not and could not bring about restoration of a sense of dignity to that class alone. In this context, we see that the sense of dignity of the petite bourgeoisie class depends on the objective moral and social feeling of each individual, on his subjective attitude towards the two poles of the colonial conflict, between which he is forced to live out the daily drama of colonialization. This drama is the more shattering to the extent to which the petite bourgeoisie in fulfilling its role is made to live alongside both the foreign dominating class and the masses. On one side the petite bourgeoisie is the victim of frequent if not daily humiliation by the foreigner, and on the other side it is aware of the injustice to which the masses are subjected and of their resistance and spirit of rebellion. Hence, arises the apparent paradox of colonal domination; it is from within the indigenous *petite bourgeoisie,* a social class which grows from colonialism itself, that arise the first important steps towards mobilizing and organizing the masses for the struggle against the colonial power.

The struggle, in the face of all kinds of obstacles and in a variety of forms, reflects the awareness or grasp of a complete identity, generalizes and consolidates the sense of dignity, strengthened by the development of political awareness, and derives from the culture or cultures of the masses in revolt one of its principal strengths.

Inside liberated Guine. (PAIGC)

Mother and child listening to address by member of 1972 Special Mission of the UN to liberated Guine. (UN Photo/Yutaka Nagata)

Two PAIGC members taking a rest in the Balana-Kitafine Sector, liberated Guiné. (UN Photo/Yutaka Nagata)

Inside a liberated zone. (PAIGC)

Amilcar Cabral addressing an audience at Lincoln University where he received the honorary doctorate during his last visit to the United States in October 1972. (AIS/Ray Lewis)

A neighborhood youth sits in front of UN and OAU representatives at a memorial service held in Harlem, New York on January 24, 1973 for the slain Amilcar Cabral. (UN Photo/Yutaka Nagata)

Lai Seck, in charge of Security in the Cubucare Sector. (UN Photo/Yutaka Nagata)

Paula Cassama, member of a action committee, addresses a mass meeting. The local action committees are composed of five members, two of whom must be women. (AIS/Robert Van Lierop)

A third grade student at a math class at the Aerolino Lopez Cruz boarding school. At right is Chairman of the 1973 Mission of the United Nations, Sevilla-Borza, visiting liberated Guine. (UN Photo/Yutaka Nagata)

People of the Cubucare Sector. (UN Photo/Yutaka Nagata)

Connecting
the Struggles:
an informal talk with Black Americans

During his last visit to the United States Cabral asked the Africa Information Service to organize a small informal meeting at which he could speak with representatives of different black organizations. The A.I.S. contacted approximately thirty organizations and on October 20, 1972, more than 120 people representing a wide range of black groups in America crowded into a small room to meet with Amilcar Cabral. A number of the people present came to New York specifically for this meeting. At the meeting, the vitality, warmth and humor of Cabral the person became evident to those who had not met him before. Parts of the discussion have been edited (gramatically) to compensate for the fact that although Cabral spoke many languages, English was not his most comfortable language.

I am bringing to you—our African brothers and sisters of the United States—the fraternal salutations of our people in assuring you we are very conscious that all in this life concerning you also concerns us. If we do not always pronounce words that clearly show this, it doesn't mean that we are not conscious of it. It is a reality and considering that the world is being made smaller each day all people are becoming conscious of this fact.

Naturally if you ask me between brothers and comrades what

I prefer—if we are brothers it is not our fault or our responsibility. But if we are comrades, it is a political engagement. Naturally we like our brothers but in our conception it is better to be a brother *and* a comrade. We like our brothers very much, but we think that if we are brothers we have to realize the responsibility of this fact and take clear positions about our problems in order to see if beyond this condition of brothers, we are also comrades. This is very important for us.

We try to understand your situation in this country. You can be sure that we realize the difficulties you face, the problems you have and your feelings, your revolts, and also your hopes. We think that our fighting for Africa against colonialism and imperialism is a proof of understanding of your problem and also a contribution for the solution of your problems in this continent. Naturally the inverse is also true. All the achievements toward the solution of your problems here are real contributions to our own struggle. And we are very encouraged in our struggle by the fact that each day more of the African people born in America become conscious of their responsibilities to the struggle in Africa.

Does that mean you have to all leave here and go fight in Africa? We do not believe so. That is not being realistic in our opinion. History is a very strong chain. We have to accept the limits of history but not the limits imposed by the societies where we are living. There is a difference. We think that all you can do here to develop your own conditions in the sense of progress, in the sense of history and in the sense of the total realization of your aspirations as human beings is a contribution for us. It is also a contribution for you to never forget that you are Africans.

Does that mean that we are racists? No! We are not racists. We are fundamentally and deeply against any kind of racism. Even when people are subjected to racism we are against racism from those who have been oppressed by it. In our opinion—not from dreaming but from a deep analysis of the real conditions of the existence of mankind and of the division of societies—racism is a result of certain circumstances. It is not eternal in any latitude in the world. It is the result of historical and economic conditions. And we can not answer racism with racism. It is not possible. In our country, despite some racist manifestations by the Portuguese, we are not fighting against the Portuguese people or whites. We are fighting for the freedom of our people—to free our people and to allow them to be able to love any kind of human being. You can not love if you are a slave. It is very difficult.

In combatting racism we don't make progress if we combat the people themselves. We have to combat the causes of racism. If a bandit comes in my house and I have a gun I can not shoot the shadow of this bandit. I have to shoot the bandit. Many people lose energy and effort, and make sacrifices combatting shadows. We have to combat the material reality that produces the shadow. If we can not change the light that is one cause of the shadow, we can at least change the body. It is important to avoid confusion between the shadow and the body that projects the shadow. We are encouraged by the fact that each day more of our people, here and in Africa, realize this reality. This reinforces our confidence in our final victory.

The fact that you follow our struggle and are interested in our achievements is good for us. We base our struggle on the concrete realities of our country. We appreciate the experiences and achievements of other peoples and we study them. But revolution or national liberation struggle is like a dress which must be fit to each individual's body. Naturally, there are certain general or universal laws, even scientific laws for any condition, but the liberation struggle has to be developed according to the specific conditions of each country. This is fundamental.

The specific conditions to be considered include—economic, cultural, social, political and even geographic. The guerrilla manuals once told us that without mountains you can not make guerrilla war. But in my country there are no mountains, only the people. In the economic field we committed an error. We began training our people to commit sabotage on the railroads. When they returned from their training we remembered that there were no railroads in our country. The Portuguese built them in Mozambique and Angola but not in our country.

There are other conditions to consider as well. You must consider the type of society in which you are fighting. Is it divided along horizontal lines or vertical lines? Some people tell us our struggle is the *same* as that of the Vietnamese people. It is *similar* but it is not the same. The Vietnamese are a people that hundreds of years ago fought against foreign invaders like a nation. We are now forging our nation in the struggle. This is a big difference. It is difficult to imagine what a difference that makes. Vietnam is also a society with clear social structures with classes well defined. There is no national bourgeoisie in our country. A miserable small petit bourgeoisie yes, but not a national bourgeoisie. These differences are very important.

Once I discussed politics with Eldridge Cleaver. He is a clever man, very intelligent. We agreed on many things but we disagreed on one thing. He told me your condition is a colonial condition. In certain aspects it seems to be, but it is not really a colonial condition. The colonial condition demands certain factors. One important factor is continuity of territories. There are others which you can see when you analyze. Many times we are confronted with phenomenon that seem to be the same, but political activity demands that we be able to distinguish them. That is not to say that the *aims* are not the same. And, that is not to say that even some of the *means* cannot be the same. However, we must deeply analyze each situation to avoid loss of time and energy doing things that we are not to do and forgetting things that we have to do.

In our country we have been fighting for nearly ten years. If we consider the changes achieved in that time, principally in the relationship between men and women, it has been more than 100 years. If we were only shooting bullets and shells, yes, ten years is too much. But we were not only doing this. We were forging a nation during these years. How long did it take the European nations to be formed—ten centuries from the middle ages to the renaissance. (Here in the United States you are still forging a nation—it is not yet completed, in my opinion. Several things have contributed to the forming and changing of this country, such as the Vietnam war, though unfortunately at the expense of the Vietnamese people. But you know the details of change in this country more than myself.)

Ten years ago, we were Fula, Mandjak, Mandinka, Balante, Pepel, and others. Now we are a nation of Guineans. Tribal divisions were one reason the Portuguese thought it would not be possible for us to fight. During these ten years we were making more and more changes, so that today we can see that there is a new man and a new woman, born with our new nation and because of our fight. This is because of our ability to fight as a nation.

Naturally, we are not defending the armed fight. Maybe I deceive people, but I am not a great defender of the armed fight. I am myself very conscious of the sacrifices demanded by the armed fight. It is a violence against even our own people. But it is not our invention—it is not our cool decision; it is the requirement of history. This is not the first fight in our country, and it is not Cabral who invented the struggle. We are following the example given by our grandfathers who fought against Portuguese domination 50 years ago. Today's fight is a continuation of the fight to defend our dignity, our right to have an identity—our own identity.

If it were possible to solve this problem without the armed fight—why not!?! But while the armed fight demands sacrifices, it also has advantages. Like everything else in the world, it has two faces—one positive the other negative—the problem is in the balance. For us now, it [the armed fight] is a good thing in our opinion, and our condition is a good thing because this armed fight helped us to accelerate the revolution of our people, to create a new situation that will facilitate our progress.

In these ten years we liberated about three-fourths of the country and we are effectively controlling two-thirds of our country. We have much work to do, but we have our state, we have a strong political organization, a developing administration, and we have created many services—always while facing the bombs of the Portuguese. That is to say, bombs *used* by the Portuguese, but made in the United States. In the military field we realized good things during these ten years. We have our national army and our local militias. We have even been able to receive a number of visitors—journalists, film-makers, scientists, teachers, writers, government representatives, and others. We also received a special mission of the United Nations last April which made a very good report about the situation in our country.

However, through this armed fight, we realized other things more important than the size of the liberated regions or the capacity of our fighters, such as the irreversible change in the attitudes of our men. We have more sacrifices to make and more difficulties to overcome, but our people are now accustomed to this, and know that for freedom we must pay a price. What can we consider better than freedom? It is not possible—nothing compares with freedom. During the visit of the Special Mission

79

of the UN to our country, one of the official observers, while on a long march, asked a small boy if he ever got tired. The boy answered, "I can't get tired—this is my country. Only the Portuguese soldiers get tired."

Now we can accelerate the process of the liberation of the rest of our country. Each day, we get more and better workers. Now we need more ammunition in order to give greater impact to our attacks against the Portuguese positions. Instead of attacking with 80 shells, we have to attack with 800, if not 2,000, and we are preparing to do this. The situation is now better in the urban centers. We are dominating the urban centers in spite of the Portuguese occupation. Links with our underground organization in these centers are now very good, and we have decided to develop our action inside these centers. We told this on the radio to the Portuguese. We told all of the people because the Portuguese cannot stop us. We told them before they would be afraid, and they are. They are even afraid of their shadows.

Another very positive aspect of our struggle is the political situation on the Cape Verde Islands. Some days ago, there were riots between our people and the police. This is a sign that great developments are coming within the framework of our fight on the Islands.

We have taken all measures demanded by the struggle, in the political as well as the military field. With the general election just completed in the liberated region, we are now creating our National Assembly. Naturally we are not doing a National Assembly like the Congress you have here or the British Parliament. All these are very important steps in accelerating the end of the colonial war in my country and for its total liberation.

We have decided to formally proclaim our state, and we hope that our brothers and sisters here, our brothers and sisters in Africa, and our friends all over the world, will take the necessary position of support for our new initiatives in this political field. In an armed fight like ours, all the political aspects have been stressed. They are stressed naturally when you approach the end. It is a dialectical process. In the beginning the fight is political only, it is then followed by the transformation into the armed stage. Step by step, the political aspect returns but at a different level, the level of the solution.

I am not going to develop these things further, I think it is better if you ask questions. We are very happy to be with you, our brothers and sisters. I tell you frankly, although it might hurt my visit to the United Nations, each day I feel myself more identified with you. I am not racist, but each day I realize that if I did not have to do what I have to do in my country, maybe I would come here to join you.

I am at your disposal for any kind of question; no secrets, or ceremonies or diplomacy with you.

QUESTION: I am from Mali. I don't know how comfortable you will be with this question, but given the nature of the fight you have been leading, are you satisfied with the type of moral, political and military aid you have been receiving from other African countries?

CABRAL: First of all, let me say to my brother, that I am comfortable with any kind of question—there is no problem. Secondly, when one is in a condition that he has to receive aid, he is never satisfied. The condition of people who are obliged by circumstances to ask for and receive aid, is to never be satisfied. If you are satisfied it is finished, you don't need aid.

Thirdly, we have to also consider the situation of the people who are helping us. You know the political and economic circumstances conditioning the attitudes of the African countries. It's true the past decade of the sixties was a great achievement for Africa—the independence of Africa. But we are not of this tree of independence of Africa. We must take our independence with force and our position is to never ask for the aid we need. We let each people give us the aid they can, and we never accept conditions with the aid. If you can give us aid like this, O.K. we are satisfied. If you can give more, we are more satisfied.

I have said to the African heads of state many times, that the aid from Africa is very useful, but not sufficient. We believe that they could do better, and so do they. Last June in the Rabat summit meetings [of the OAU] they agreed to increase their aid by 50 percent. Why didn't they do this before? We know that they had not only financial and economic difficulties, but political difficulties as well. In some cases, the difficulty was a lack of consciousness about the importance of this problem. But each day they are realizing more and maybe when they fully realize the importance of this problem we will all be independent.

QUESTION: I would like to know what forward thrust your

country would have in the absence of NATO support, that this country gives, and what the arguments are that the U.S. offers for its participation in NATO which we all know is the conduit which supplies the Portuguese with their arms? This is something which we can take immediate political action on.

CABRAL: You see, Portugal is an underdeveloped country—the most backward in Western Europe. It is a country that doesn't even produce toy planes—this is not a joke, it's true. Portugal would never be able to launch three colonial wars in Africa without the help of NATO, the weapons of NATO, the planes of NATO, the bombs of NATO—it would be impossible for them. This is not a matter for discussion. The Americans know it, the British know it, the French know it very well, the West Germans also know it, and the Portuguese also know it very well.

We cannot talk of American participation in NATO, because NATO is the creation of the United States. Once I came here to the U.S. and I was invited to lunch by the representative of the U.S. on the United Nations' Fourth Committee. He was also the deputy chief of the U.S. delegation to the United Nations. I told him we are fighting against Portuguese colonialism, and not asking for the destruction of NATO. We don't think it is necessary to destroy NATO in order to free our country. But why is the U.S. opposing this? He told me that he did not agree with this policy [U.S. support of NATO] but that there is a problem of world security and in the opinion of his government it is necessary to give aid to Portugal in exchange for use of the Azores as a military base. Acceptance of Portuguese policy is necessary for America's global strategy, he explained.

I think he was telling me the truth, but only part of the truth because the U.S. also supports Portugal in order to continue the domination of Africa, if not over other parts of the world. I must clarify that this man left his position in the U.N. and during his debate in the U.S. Congress took a clear position favorable to ours and asked his government many times to stop its aid to Portugal, but the government didn't accept.

What is the justification for this? There is no justification—no justification at all. It is U.S. imperialism. Portugal is an appendage of imperialism, a rotten appendage of imperialism. You know that Portugal is a semi-colony itself. Since 1775 Portugal has been a semi-colony of Britain. This is the only reason that Portugal was able to preserve the colonies during the partition of Africa. How could this poor miserable country preserve the colonies in the face of the ambitions and jealousies of Germany, France, England, Belgium, and the emerging American imperialism? It was because England adopted a tactic. It said— Portugal is my colony, if it preserves colonies they are also my colonies—and England defended the interests of Portugal with force. But now it is not the same. Angola is not really a Portuguese colony. Mozambique is not really a Portuguese colony. You can see the statistics. More than 60 percent of the principal exports of Angola are not for Portugal. Approximately the same percentage of the investments in Angola and Mozambique are not Portuguese, and each day this is increasing. Guinea and Cape Verde are very poor and do not have very good climates. They are the only Portuguese colonies. Portugal is, principally for Angola and Mozambique, the policeman and the receiver of taxes. But they will not tell you this.

QUESTION: My question concerns the basis of law you are using in your country. Are you using the laws of the Portuguese in terms of the National Assembly? What kinds of criteria are you going to use?

CABRAL: If Portugal had created in my country an Assembly, we would not create one ourselves. We don't accept any institution of the Portuguese colonialists. We are not interested in the preservation of any of the structures of the colonial state. It is our opinion that it is necessary to totally destroy, to break, to reduce to ash all aspects of the colonial state in our country in order to make everything possible for our people. The masses realize that this is true, in order to convince everyone we are really finished with colonial domination in our country.

Some independent African states preserved the structures of the colonial state. In some countries they only replaced a white man with a black man, but for the people it is the same. You have to realize that it is very difficult for the people to make a distinction between one Portuguese, or white, administrator and one black administrator. For the people it is the administrator that is fundamental. And the principle—if this administrator, a black one is living in the same house, with the same gestures, with the same car, or sometimes a better one, what is the difference? The nature of the state we have to create in our country is a very good question for it is a fundamental one.

Our fortune is that we are creating the state through the

struggle. We now have popular tribunals—people's courts—in our country. We cannot create a judicial system like the Portuguese in our country because it was a colonial one, nor can we even make a copy of the judicial system in Portugal—it is impossible. Through the struggle we created our courts and the peasants participate by electing the courts themselves. Ours is a new judicial system, totally different from any other system, born in our country through the struggle. It is similar to other systems, like the one in Vietnam, but it is also different because it corresponds to the conditions of our country.

If you really want to know the feelings of our people on this matter I can tell you that our government and all its institutions have to take another nature. For example, we must not use the houses occupied by the colonial power in the way they used them. I proposed to our party that the government palace in Bissau be transformed into a people's house for culture, not for our prime minister or something like this (I don't believe we will have prime ministers anyway). This is to let the people realize that they conquered colonialism—it's finished this time—it's not only a question of a change of skin. *This is really very important. It is the most important problem in the liberation movement. The problem of the nature of the state created after independence is perhaps the secret of the failure of African independence.*

QUESTION: Looking at Africa geographically, where does the PAIGC get most of its support, North Africa, or Sub-Saharan Africa, and in a broader sense, how does support from China and Russia compare?

CABRAL: We don't like this division of Africa. We have the support of the OAU for some years now. We have the total support of the OAU. All the African countries support the PAIGC, no exceptions of any voice against us. And through the OAU, the Liberation Committee gives us financial help. There are some African countries, maybe not more than the fingers on my hand, that help us directly, also. With them we have bilateral relations. Some are in the north, others in the west, and others in the east.

About China and the Soviet Union, we always had the support of the socialist countries—moral, political and material. Some have given more material support than others. Until now the country that has helped us the most is the Soviet Union, and we said it many times before all kinds of meetings. Until now they've helped us the most in supplying materials for the war. If you want to verify this you can come to my country and see. This is the situation.

QUESTION: My question is about the role of women. What is the nature of their transformation from the old system under imperialism?

CABRAL: In our country you find many societies with different traditions and rules on the role of women. For example, in the Fula society a woman is like a piece of property of the man, the owner of the home. This is the typical patriarchal society. But even there women have dignity, and if you enter the house you would see that inside the house, the woman is the chief. On the other hand, in the Balante society women have more freedom.

To understand these differences you have to know that in the Fula society all that is produced belongs to the father. In the Balante society all that is produced belongs to the people that work and women work very hard so they are free. It is very simple. But the problem is about the political role in the fight. You know that in our country there were even matriarchal societies where women were the most important element. On the Bijagos Islands they had queens. They were not queens because they were the daughters of kings. They had queens succeeding queens. The religious leaders were women too. Now they are changing.

I tell you these things so that you can understand our society better. But during the fight the important thing is the political role of women. Yes, we have made great achievements, but not enough. We are very far from what we want to do, but this is not a problem that can be solved by Cabral signing a decree. It is all a part of the process of transformation, of change in the material conditions of the existence of our people, but also in the minds of the women, because sometimes the greatest difficulty is not only in the men but in the women too.

We have a big problem with our nurses, because we trained about three hundred nurses—women—but they married, they get children and for them it's finished. This is very bad. For some this doesn't happen. Carmen Pereira, for instance, is a nurse, and she is also a member of the high political staff of the Party. She is responsible for all social and cultural problems in the southern liberated region. She's a member of the Executive Committee of the Party. There are many others too, trained not only in the country but in the exterior also, in foreign countries. But we have much work to do.

In the beginning of the struggle, when we launched the guerrilla struggle, young women came without being called and asked for weapons to fight, hundreds and hundreds. But step by step some problems came in this framework and we had to distribute, to partition the war. Today, women are principally in what you call the local armed forces and in the political war—working on health problems, and instruction also.

I hope we can send some of our women here so you will be able to know them. But we have big problems to solve and we have a great problem with some of the leaders of the Party. We have (even myself) to combat ourselves on this problem, because we have to be able to cut this cultural element, with its great roots, until the day we put down this bad thing—the exploitation of women, but we made great progress in this field in these ten years.

QUESTION: Comrade Cabral, you spoke about universal scientific laws of revolution. It is very clear that in this country, we too, are engaged in some stage of development of a revolutionary struggle. Certainly one of the most controversial aspects of our struggle is the grasp of these scientific universal laws. Would you, therefore, talk about your Party's understanding of revolutionary theory, particularly as related to Cuba, China, the Soviet Union, and the anti-colonial wars of national liberation? It is very clear that on the international level there are defined positions being taken that are probably more important in countries, and with parties, which have defined positions than they are in our struggle which is so fractured that we play little part in this international struggle for the clarification of these universal scientific laws. So I wonder, would you speak on this problem?

CABRAL: You see, I think that all kinds of struggle for liberation obey a group of laws. The application of these laws to a certain case depends on the nature of the case. Maybe all these laws are applicable, but maybe only some, maybe only one, it depends. In science you know water boils at 100° C. It's a law. Naturally, with the condition that we are speaking in centigrade degrees, this is a specification. What does it mean if we are measuring fahrenheit—it's not the same. And this is also only at sea level. When you go up in the mountains this law is not true. Newton and many others told us it is the same but Einstein demonstrated that it is not always true. It is sometimes more complex.

It's the same in the field of the scientific character of the liberation struggle. Cuba, Soviet Union, China, Viet Nam, and so on—our country, are different entities in this context. Sometimes you can even explain conflicts between their people because of the different nature of their struggle, dictated by the different conditions of the countries—historical, economical, and so on.

I have to tell you that when we began preparing for our struggle in our own country, we didn't know Mao Tse-tung. The first time I faced a book of Mao Tse-tung was in 1960. Our party was created in 1956. We knew less about the struggle of Cuba, but later we tried to know the experiences of other peoples. Some experiences we put aside because the difference was so great that it would waste time to study them. We think the experiences of other people is very important for you, principally to know things you should not do. Because what you have to do in your country you have to create yourself.

The general laws are very simple. For instance, the development of the armed fight in a country characterized by agriculture where most, if not all, of the population are peasants means you have to do the struggle as in China, in Viet Nam or in my country. Maybe you begin in the towns, but you recognize that this is not good. You pass to the countryside to mobilize the peasants. You recognize that the peasants are very difficult to mobilize under certain conditions, but you launch the armed struggle and step by step you approach the towns in order to finish the colonists.

For instance, this is scientific: in the colonial war there is a contradiction. What is it? It is that the colonial power in order to really dominate the country has to disperse its forces. In dispersing its forces it becomes weak—the national forces can destroy them. As you begin to destroy them they are obliged to concentrate, but when they concentrate they leave areas of the country you can control, administer and create structures in. Then they can never destroy you. It's always possible. You can tell me it's not possible in the United States, the United States is not an agricultural country like this. But if you study deeply the conditions in your country maybe you will find that this law is also applicable. This is what I can tell you, because it is a very big problem to discuss, if I understood your question.

QUESTION (cont'd): I'd like to rephrase part of it. What I'm trying to get at is how, in setting up the cadre training school that you set up in Conakry, did you have access to the revolutionary experiences of the countries I mentioned? What kind of literature did you read? The point that I am trying to drive at is not the form of waging a revolutionary struggle. I understand the differences in concrete conditions. I want to know how one moves through a colonial or a semi-feudal condition into socialism—how the experience of moving from capitalism into socialism (clearly the dominant revolutionary experience in the world) was gained—how you were able to set up a training program in which cadre were exposed to this information?

CABRAL: In the beginning we established in Conakry what you call a political school for militants. About one thousand people came from our country by groups. We first asked—who are we? Where are we? What do we want? How do we live? What is our enemy? Who is this enemy? What can he do against us? What is our country? Where is our country?—things like this, step by step, explaining our real conditions and explaining what we want, why we want it and why we had to fight against the Portuguese. Among all these people some step by step, approached other experiences. But the problem of going from feudal or semi-feudal society or tribal society to socialism is a very big problem, even from capitalism to socialism.

If there are Marxists here they know that Marx said that capitalism created all the conditions for socialism. The conditions were created but never passed. Even then it is very difficult. This is even more reason for the feudal or semi-feudal tribal societies to jump to socialism—but it's not a problem of jumping. It's a process of development. You have to establish the political aims and based on your own condition the ideological content of the fight. To have ideology doesn't necessarily mean that you have to define whether you are communist, socialist, or something like this. To have ideology is to know what you want in your own condition.

We want in our country this: to have no more exploitation of our people, not by white people or by black peple. We don't want any more exploitation. It is in this way we educate our people—the masses, the cadres, the militants—in this way. For that we are taking step by step, all the measures necessary to avoid this exploitation. How? We give to our people the instrument to control, the people lead. And we give to our people all possibility to participate more actively each day in the direction of their own life.

Naturally, if an American comes he may say you are doing socialism in your country. This is a responsibility for him. We are not preoccupied with labels you see. We are occupied in the content of the thing, what we are doing, how we are doing it, what chances are we creating for realizing this aim. There are some societies that passed from feudal or semi-feudal stages to being socialist societies. But one of their specifics was having a state imposing this passage. We do not have this. We have to create for ourselves the instruments of the state inside our country, in the conditions of our history, in order to orientate all to a life of justice, work for progress and equality. Equality of chance for all people is the problem. The problem of equality is equality of chance. This is what I can tell you. This is a very big discussion, philosophical if you want something like this.

QUESTION: What direct relationship does the OAU have with your party? You mentioned the OAU several times and I heard some things about the OAU, but I wanted to know whether or not it has been helpful to you and, if it has, in what ways?

CABRAL: Yes, they are good relations. Now we can even tell that we are nearly members of the OAU, because at the last summit conference in Rabat, they admitted the recognized liberation movements, like my party, to participate in the debate concerning their own cases. The relations are very good. We have the help of the OAU, like I said—not enough we think, but they are trying to increase this help and we think that in our own case, maybe next year, we will be a member, full member of the OAU.

QUESTION: (cont'd) Why? Do you see it as the organization for Africa?

CABRAL: A real organization for Africa? It depends. Now at this stage of the revolution in Africa, the OAU is a very good thing. It is such a good thing that imperialism is doing its best to finish it. Naturally, maybe for your ideas the OAU doesn't

answer well, doesn't fully correspond to your hopes. Maybe you
are right, but this is not the problem. In the political field, you
have to know at each stage if you are doing the possible or not,
and preparing the field for the possible for tomorrow or not.
This is the problem.
QUESTION (cont'd) Yes, but how was it created and how is
it being supported?
CABRAL: Oh, that's a very big matter. You don't know how
it was created? They met in May in 1963 in Addis Ababa, and
they established a charter.
QUESTION (cont'd) Who is supporting this organization?
CABRAL: Who is supporting it? The states—the African states?
Yes the African states. The imperialists—no, you are not right.
You are not right, my sister, We can tell that some of the Afri-
can states . . . (interrupted)
QUESION: (cont'd) If there is such an organization why are
we still where we are? It is just the leaders that elect to go there,
not the kind of people like yourself, who are coming down to
the masses and speaking the truth. These are neo-colonial
leaders.
CABRAL: No. But that is not the problem. You are confused.
You are making a mistake. One problem is the problem of
OAU. The OAU is an organization of African states, it's true.
The African states pay to the OAU their respective dues, it's
true. Are imperialists supporting the OAU? On the contrary,
they do their best not to because there is a potential danger for
them. The other problem is: are these African states all really
independent? Some of them are neo-colonialist, but you have
to distinguish this thing in order to do something. If you confuse
all—it's not possible.
QUESTION (cont'd) But brother, why is it that each time the
question of Pan-Africanism is brought to the discussion most
of them take different views?
CABRAL: Oh yes. You see you cannot demand all the African
states to agree immediately on Pan-Africanism. Even if we discuss Pan-Africanism you would be surprised. I am for Pan-Africanism. I am for African unity. But we have to be for these
things and do them when possible, not to do it now. You see,
my sister, you here in the United States, we understand you.
You are for Pan-Africanism and you want it today. Pan-Africanism now! We are in Africa; don't confuse this reaction

against Pan-Africanism with the situation of the OAU. I can tell you, the head of state in Africa I admired the most in my life was Nkrumah.

QUESTION: (cont'd) He was the only one. He was the father.

CABRAL: Nkrumah was not the father of Pan-Africanism. An American, DuBois, was the father, if you want. Pan-Africanism is a means to return to the source. You see, it's a very big problem. It's not like this. You are looking at the surface. It's not like this. Nkrumah told me in Conakry—(unfortunately he is not alive, but I am not lying, I never lied in my life) he was one of my best friends, I'll never forget him; and you can read my speech at his memorial—you see he told me, "Cabral, I tell you one thing, our problem of African unity is very important, really, but now if I had to begin again, my approach would be different."

Unfortunately, I am leaving, but if not I would like very much to speak with you in order to show you Pan-Africanism is a very nice idea; but we have to work for it, and it is not for me to accuse Houphouet-Boigny or Mobuto, because they don't want it. They cannot want it! It is more difficult for some heads of state in Africa to accept African unity as defined by Nkrumah than it is for them to come here to the most racist of the white racists and tell them to accept equal rights for all Africa. You see, more difficult. It's a great problem, my sister. And we think on this problem every day because our future concerns that.

We have a meeting at half past seven with the Chairman of the Decolonization Committee. We have to go there. It is about 20 minutes from here. I am late.

QUESTION: When will we see you again?

CABRAL: Again? I never know. It is difficult for me but I hope in two years. Also for some of you, if you want, you can come to my country and see me and see our people.

QUESTION: How?

CABRAL: By paying the travel. [laughter]

QUESTION: What are some of the specific financial and political things we can do to further the struggle?

CABRAL: Personally I don't agree with that question. I think that this meeting is a meeting of brothers and sisters. You represent several organizations. I am very glad because we want your unity. We know it's very difficult—it's more difficult to make your unity than Pan-Africanism maybe. But we would like you to consider this meeting a meeting between brothers and sisters trying to reinforce not only our links in blood, and in history, but also in aims. I am very glad to have been here with you and I deeply regret that it is not possible to be with you longer. Thank you very much.

New Year's Message

This is the New Year's Message of January, 1973, delivered by Cabral to the PAIGC. It was the last written statement by Cabral to the people of Guine and the Cape Verde Islands. In that respect it is the political testament of Amilcar Cabral. In this document he analyzes what progress has been made and the nature of the struggle yet to come.

Comrades, Compatriots,

At this time, as we commemorate a new year of life and struggle, and a year in which our people's fight for independence is ten years old, I must remind everyone—militants, fighters, leaders and responsible people in our Party—that it is time for action and not words. Action that must daily become more vigorous and effective in Guine in order to inflict greater defeats on the Portuguese colonialists, and to remove all their vain and criminal pretensions of reconquering our country. Action, too, that must develop daily and become more organized in the Cape Verde islands, so as to lead the struggle into a new phase, in harmony with the aspirations of our people and the requirements of the total liberation of our country.

I wish, however, to respect tradition by addressing a few words to you at a time when all sane people—those who want peace, liberty and happiness for all men—renew their hopes and belief in a better life for humanity, belief in dignity and in the independence and progress of all peoples.

RETURN TO THE SOURCE

As everyone knows, in the past year we have achieved general elections in the liberated areas, with universal suffrage and a secret vote, for the creation of Regional Councils and the first National Assembly in the history of our people. In all sectors of all the regions the elections were conducted in an atmosphere of great enthusiasm among the population. The electorate voted massively from the lists that had been prepared throughout eight months of public and democratic debates, in the course of which the representatives for each sector were selected. Once assembled the elected Regional Councils elected, in their turn, representatives to the National Popular Assembly from among their members. This will have 120 members, of which 80 will have been drawn from the popular masses and 40 from the political cadres, the military, the technicians and others of the Party. As you know, the representatives of the sectors temporarily occupied by the colonialists have been chosen provisionally.

And so, today, our African Peoples of Guine possess a new means of sovereignty: their National Assembly. This will be, in accordance with the constitution we are preparing, the supreme medium of the sovereignty of our people in Guine. Tomorrow, with the certain advance of the struggle, we will create in the same way the first National Popular Assembly of the Cape Verde islands. The combined meeting of the members of these two organs will constitute the Supreme Assembly of the People of Guine and the Cape Verde islands.

The creation of the first National Popular Assembly in Guine is a victory that transcends even the difficult but glorious struggle of our people for independence. It opens new perspectives for the progress of our politico-military action; it is the result, of the effort and willing sacrifice of our people through ten years of armed struggle; it is a concrete proof of the sovereignty of our people and of their high level of patriotic and national consciousness. I wish, therefore, at this time, to warmly congratulate our people and all of the electorate who, as conscious men and women, have been able to accomplish their duty as free citizens of our African nation with such dignity. I wish to congratulate also all the militants, organizers and leaders who, in electoral committees or in other kinds of activities, have contributed to the success of this venture, the achievement of which will live in the history of our country. I congratulate the brave fighters of our armed forces with equal enthusiasm; by their courageous action they have created in all sectors the security needed for holding the elections, despite the criminal attempts of the colonialist enemy to stop them taking place.

A National Assembly, however, like any organ in any living body, must be able to function in order to justify its existence. We thus have a major task ahead of us, to be accomplished within the framework of our struggle in this new year of 1973: we must make our National Popular Assembly work. And this we shall do, thereby implementing the decisions taken by our great Party at the meeting of the Supreme Council of the Struggle held in August 1971, decisions which are upheld by the people with great enthusiasm.

In the course of this coming year and as soon as it is conveniently possible, we shall call a meeting of the National Popular Assembly in Guine in order to accomplish the first historic mission incumbent upon it: the proclamation of our State, the creation of an Executive for this State and the promulgation of a fundamental Law—the first Constitution in our history—which will be the basis of the active life of our African nation. That is to say: legitimate representatives of our people, chosen by the people and freely elected by patriotic and responsible citizens of our country, will proceed with the most important act of their lives and in the lives of our people: that of stating to the world that our African Nation, forged in the struggle, has irreversibly decided to move towards independence without waiting for the consent of the Portuguese colonialists, and that, dating from this statement, the Executive of our State will be, under the direction of our Party, the PAIGC, the only true and legitimate representative of our people in everything, national and international, that concerns it.

We are moving from the position of a colony which has a Liberation Movement and of which the people have already liberated, in ten years of armed struggle, the greater part of its national territory, to the position of a country which runs its own State and which has a part of its national territory occupied by foreign armed forces.

This radical change in the situation in our country corresponds to the concrete reality of the life and struggle of our people in Guine; is based on the concrete results of our struggle and has the firm support of all African peoples and governments, as well as that of the anti-colonialist and anti-racist forces of the world. It also adheres to the principles of the United Nations Charter and to the resolutions adopted by this international organization, notably in its 27th session.

Nothing, no criminal action or illusionist manoeuvre by the Portuguese colonialists can stop our African people, masters of their own destinies and aware of their rights and duties, from taking this decisive and transcendent step towards the achievement of the fundamental objective of our struggle: the conquest of national independence and the building, in restored peace and dignity, of its true advancement under the exclusive direction of its own children beneath the glorious flag of our Party.

The particular importance of the formation of the National Popular Assembly, of the proclamation of the State of Guine and of the creation of its corresponding executive membership, who will be neither provisional, neither will they live in exile, necessarily implies much greater responsbilities for our people, and in particular for the militants, the fighters, the organisers and the leaders of our Party. These historic undertakings demand greater effort and daily sacrifice on our part, further thought to ensure better action, further activity to ensure better thought. We must think about each specific problem that we have to resolve in such a way as to find the best solution for it under the particular conditions of our country and our struggle. These undertakings also require that we intensify and further develop our political and military action in Guine without, however, neglecting the important activities that we are carrying out in the economic, social and cultural fields. They demand that we successfully deploy the necessary effort for the advance of the political struggle in the Cape Verde islands and in order that our people should as soon as possible move into systematic direct action against the Portuguese colonialists.

Under these conditions we cannot for one moment forget that we are at war and that the main enemy of our people and of Africa—the fascist Portuguese colonialists—still nourish, with the blood and misery of their people and by underhand manoeuvres and savage acts, the criminal intention and vain hope of destroying our Party, of annihilating our struggle and recolonizing our people. Our attention and the best of our energy and effort must be devoted to the armed struggle, to war, to concrete action by both our local and our national armed forces. We must also, in 1973, set in motion all our human and material capability and ability in order to inject even greater intensity into the struggle on all fronts and extract the greatest profit from men, arms and the experience we have, thereby to inflict even greater blows on the colonialist enemy by destroying an even larger number of their living forces. For the history of colonial warfare as well as our own experience over ten years of struggle have taught us that the colonial aggressors—and the Portuguese colonial aggressors in particular —only understand the language of force and only measure reality by the number of corpses.

It is true that in 1972 we inflicted great defeats and important losses on the Portuguese aggressors. In a few days our Information Service will publish the account of our actions over the past year, which will be widely reported by our broadcasting station "Radio Libertacao" as well as by other means of information. But we must recognize that the enemy, possessing more planes and helicopters provided by its allies in NATO, has significantly increased its bombing and terrorist raids against our liberated regions; it has attempted and still tries to create difficult conditions for us with its plots for the reoccupation of a certain number of localities in these regions. Above all, we must recognize that with the manpower, arms and experience that we possess we could and should have done more and better. This is what we must do and certainly will do in 1973, especially as we are going to use more powerful arms and other instruments of war on all fronts.

Basing ourselves on a greater number of better trained cadres and fighters, strengthened by greater experience, we are going to make more efficient use of all the means presently at our disposal, and of those that we will have in the future, inflicting decisive and mortal blows on the criminal colonialists.

Parallel to our intensification of armed action on all fronts we must be capable of developing our action behind and at the heart of the enemy, and where it feels itself to be most secure. I wish to congratulate the courageous militants who by their decisive action, have inflicted some important blows against the enemy over the past year, particularly in Bissau, Bafata and Bula. But I also draw everyone's attention to the need to develop and intensify this kind of action.

In fact the time has come when, based on solid and efficient clandestine organization, there should be the destruction of the greatest possible number of the human and material assets of the Portuguese colonialists in the urban centres of our country. In fact we are facing a savage enemy which does not have the slightest scruple in its criminal activities, which has access to every possible means of attempting to destroy us wherever we are. Also, since we are fighting in our country for the sacred right of our people to independence, peace and true progress, we must at this decisive moment attack the colonialist and racist enemy—itself, its agents, its assets,—with destructive blows, wherever tney are. This is an urgent task to which all organizers and militants of this part of the struggle must dedicate themselves with the greatest attention; particularly those comrades who, with courage and decisiveness, are active in the centres and areas still occupied by the enemy.

I would like to mention here an important problem that we are facing in the colonial war; the huge attempts by the enemy to occupy or reoccupy a certain number of the localities of the liberated areas. I wish to remind the comrades of the Party and our people that these attempts, such as bombing and terrorist assaults, successful or not, are characteristic of colonial warfare. They are necessarily part of the action of the colonialist aggressor, especially when the patriotic forces have liberated the greater part of the national territory, as in our case. We must therefore face this problem realistically and give it its proper evaluation within the general context of our struggle, without either exaggerating or diminishing its importance.

As the comrades, and especially the leaders and organizers of the Party know, in the context of its colonial war the colonial aggressor is coming up against a fundamental contradiction, which has no solution and with which it struggles throughout the war. It is the following: so as to feel that it dominates the territory, it is forced to disperse its troops to enable them to occupy the greatest possible number of positions. This makes it weaker, and the concentrated patriotic forces are able to direct hard and mortal blows at it. This forces it to retreat, to enable it to concentrate its troops and try to avoid losing a great many human lives and be able to resist the advancing nationalist forces, and gain time against them. But, by concentrating its troops, its military and political presence ceases to exist over vast areas of the country, which are organized and administered by the patriotic forces.

Blinded by the despair brought on by defeats to which it has been subjected and is still subjected both in our country and internationally, in the present phase of our struggle and of the Portuguese colonial war, the enemy tries vainly to make the Corubal river return to Fouta Djalou instead of flowing towards the Goba and the sea. This attempt, like that of tricking our people with the mirage of the "Better Guine" a la Portugal, and that of making African fight African, is doomed to failure. The enemy will never free itself from the basic contradiction of its dirty colonial war.

What is important for us, with our knowledge of the strategy which the enemy is forced to use by the objective laws of colonial warfare, is not to worry too much when the enemy tries to settle in Gompara, Cabochanque, Cadique or in other places. What is important is on the one hand to carry forward our own battle plans and on the other to do our best to destroy the greatest number of living enemy forces; whenever they settle or move to take up a position in any part of our liberated areas. What counts is to aim heavy blows at them, to allow them no rest, to turn any occupied position into a graveyard for their troops, until they are forced to retreat, as we have done in Blana, Gadembel and more recently in Tabanca Nova in the Cubiseco Region. This we must do and will certainly do to any position which the enemy occupies inside the liberated areas. It is what we must also do to the barracks and entrenched camps still in our country.

Naturally, in 1973 we must continue to intensify our political work among the popular masses, both inside the liberated areas and the occupied zones of Guine, and on the Cape Verde islands. Without wishing to diminish the value of the work already done in this field, which produced the failure of the so-called "Better Guine" policy—a policy as false as the boasts that were made about it, we must recognise that there are some sectors where political action is still deficient. In this coming year we must make every effort to improve our activities in these areas for, as we know, however important our armed action is, our struggle is a thoroughly political one which aims at a specific political objective: the independence and progress of our country.

RETURN TO THE SOURCE

While I congratulate the comrades who, both in Guine and on the Cape Verde islands, have bettered their political work throughout the past year, I encourage everyone to double their efforts in consolidating and developing the political conquests of the Party and the Struggle, so that each day the political consciousness and patriotism of the masses, the militants and the fighters will be raised higher, strengthening the indestructible unity of our people, the vital basis of the success of our struggle. In this way, in the area of security and control, vigilance will be strengthened towards the enemy and their agents, against all those who because of opportunism, ambition and moral weakness or servility towards the enemy, might try to destroy our Party and consequently the just struggle of our people for independence.

On the Cape Verde islands the events of September 1972, which formed the first clash between the population of the Archipelago and the forces of colonial oppression, have once again shown the level of tension produced by the political situation. In congratulating the patriots of Praia and Santiago, who acted with courage and decisiveness in the face of provocation by the colonialists and their agents, I wish to encourage them continually to improve their clandestine organization, to act with sureness and without allowing the enemy to destroy the Nationalist cadres, and to prepare themselves by every means within their reach for the new phase of our struggle in the Archipelago, which is forced ahead by the criminal stubbornness of the Portuguese colonialists. I wish to stress that the Party executive is more determined than ever to put everything into developing the struggle on the Cape Verde islands.

Looking back on the progress already made and at the complexity of the specific problems to be solved, it has become necessary and urgent, in my opinion, to proceed with a realistic modification inside the structure of the Party to enable a certain number of comrades to devote themselves entirely to the development of the struggle on the Cape Verde islands. Such a modification will be proposed at the next meeting of the Party executive.

Still on the political front, I draw the attention of the comrades to the diversity of the new problems that we have to study in an efficient manner, problems arising from the new perspectives of the development of the struggle which will be opened up by the proclamation of the state of Guine: in the interior, improvement and development of the administrative services, creation of controlling bodies for our activities, a new census of the population with identification of all its component elements etc.; and in the exterior, organization, control and protection of emigrant citizens, their identification and a corresponding distribution of passports, mobilization for the struggle, etc. wthout going into the kinds of relations to be established on the international front. These are certainly new problems and very important ones that we must study deeply and resolve in time.

The preoccupation of war and political work must not, however, make us forget or underestimate the importance of our activities on the economic, social and cultural front which are the foundations of the new life we are creating inside the liberated regions. We must all, especially the cadres who specialize in these matters, pay our best attention to the problems of the economy, health, social welfare, education and culture, to im-improve our work significantly and be able to resolve the vast problems we have to face in this new phase of our struggle. With this in view we must now steadfastly and determinedly face up to our major concerns: the feeding of the people, the improvement of living conditions for the population, taxes, the exchequer, the new financial life which we hope to establish, the money we will use, etc. as well as the kind of social security to be evolved based on our experience, school curriculae and the forming of new centres for national reconstruction and the building of our people's progress. So many new problems, complex certainly, but invigorating, that we must resolve while we continue to intensify and develop vigorous politico-military action to expel the colonialist troops from the positions they still occupy in Guine and the Cape Verde islands. The specialist groups in the Party will have to devote their attention to the study and solution of these problems, in order to accomplish their duty towards the people.

In the name of the Party executive, I congratulate the agricultural workers of Guine for the crops they harvested last year despite the scarcity of rain. I wish to encourage them to do more and better this year to ensure a good crop for, as we know, therein lies the main base of our life and struggle and the Portuguese try to destroy it by every means in their power when they find themselves unable to steal the fruits of our people's labors.

But it is with sadness that I now remember that at this moment the population of the Cape Verde islands is menaced by famine. This is the Portuguese colonialists' fault because they have never wished nor thought to create the economic and social conditions in the Archipelago to ensure the subsistence at a decent level of the population in very dry years. Forced by the advance of the struggle and by the denunciations of the Party to the world, the fascist colonial government of Portugal granted loans and subsidies to the Cape Verde islands to, as the colonialists say, "attenuate the crisis." That is to say, in order to prevent too many people dying of starvation at one time, although without stopping the weak, especially children, from dying of specific hunger or even total starvation. I raise my voice once again in the name of the Party executive to protest against this situation and to denounce the crime perpetrated by the fascist colonial Government of Lisbon in transporting to Portugal fifteen or twenty thousand young Capeverdians to work in the mines, sweep the streets in the main cities, and do unskilled labor. This is done with the ulterior aim of barring the way to progress in our liberation struggle, causing a great loss of vital strength from the Cape Verde Islands. I appeal to all Capeverdian and Guinean patriots living in Portugal to keep in close contact and organize themselves towards uniting with all the forced laborers transferred from the Cape Verde Islands, developing their patriotic activities in the service of the Party, our people and Africa. Thus, at the right moment, they should be able to aim hard blows at the enemy with the result that the takers are in turn taken.

I draw the attention of those responsible for the revictualling of the population, especially those who work in the people's shops, to the fact that this year the Party will possess greater quantities than ever before of urgently needed articles. We must be able to place them at the disposal of the population of all the liberated areas, whatever the difficulties we may face in so doing. In fact we have received aid from socialist countries, in particular the Soviet Union, Sweden, Norway and other countries, as well as from humanitarian organizations; this aid will afford us great improvements in the functioning of the people's shops, as well as of health and educational institutions.

I hope that everyone will make the necessary effort to ensure that 1973 will be a period of greater efficiency still in the revictualling of our population in articles of primary necessity.

As everyone knows 1972 was a year of great and decisive international victories by our great Party and our people. Among the main achievements I wish to remind you of the following:

The now historic visit of the United Nations Special Mission to the liberated areas of our country, which brought great results for the prestige not only of our Party and the struggle, but also to all the African Liberation Movements. While recalling this event which the Portuguese colonial aggressors wished to oppose with their most violent crimes, I salute in this new year the peoples of Ecuador, Sweden, Tunisia, Senegal and Japan, whose courageous children visited our country as members of the special mission. I thank their respective Governments for having allowed their representatives to make such a visit, and the Secretary General of the United Nations for the firm way in which he applied a great historic resolution of the General Assembly of that international organization.

The Resolution of the Decolonization Committee of the United Nations in its session in April 1972, by which our Party was recognized by general acclamation as being the only true and legitimate representative of the peoples of Guine and the Cape Verde Islands.

The resolution of the 27th Session of the General Assembly of the United Nations which, among other vital decisions, confirmed the recognition of our Party as the sole legitimate representative of our African people and requested all the States, Governments and national and international organizations, as well as the specialized agencies of the United Nations, to reinforce their aid to our Party and to always and only deal with it in every circumstance concerning the peoples of Guine and the Cape Verde Islands.

The historic resolution of the Security Council which, under its first woman President, our Guinean sister and comrade Jeanne Martin Cisse, unanimously adopted a resolution condemning Portuguese colonialism and demanding the Portuguese Government stop the colonial war in Africa, withdraw its occupying troops and enter into negotiations with the respective patriotic forces which in our country, are represented by our Party. For the first time in the diplomatic and political struggle against Portuguese colonialism, our Party spoke at the United Nations with the status of Observer; even the allies of the fascist Colonial Government of Portugal voted in unison against it in the United Nations Security Council. This resolution has, and will have, great significance in the future development of our politico-military actions to expel the criminal Portuguese colonial aggressors.

Finally, but not least, I remember the resolutions of solidarity and unconditional total support adopted by the conference of the African heads of State and Governments in Rabat, at which our Party was once again chosen as spokesman for all the African Liberation Movements.

This past year has been full of great international victories, made more so by the fact that we are sure of the moral, political and, in some cases, material support of the independent African States. Firstly, the neighboring and fraternal countries, the Republics of Guine and Senegal, as well as that of all the anti-colonialist and anti-racial countries and forces. We have received, or are about to receive in this coming year, further material from the Soviet Union and from all the other socialist countries; from Sweden, Norway, Denmark, Finland; various Parties and political organizations in Europe and from humanitarian institutions like the World Council of Churches, Rowntree in England, the World Church Service of America, the French Popular Aid, the International Red Cross and various other support committees established around the world. Specialized or autonomous departments of the United Nations, like the African Economic Committee, UNESCO, UNICEF, WHO, the High Commission for Refugees and the ILO* are and will continue to increase their cooperation with our Party, and tomorrow, surely, with our State.

Comrades and Compatriots, you now understand why the fascist colonial Government of Marcelo Caetano and its representatives in our country find reason to despair. You will also understand why, given their unscrupulous and contemptuous attitudes towards the rights of all peoples including their own, they resort to any means and crimes with which to try and stop our struggle. You understand now why the Portuguese colonial aggressors and their leader in our country are more vicious than

---

* International Labor Organization.

ever, and intensify their bombing, multiply their assaults on our liberated areas, and make every effort to try and reoccupy a certain number of places inside these areas. It is in order to console themselves for the military, political and diplomatic defeats that we inflict upon them; it is in order to try, with every new crime they perpetrate, to demoralize our forces and demobilize our population. It is the defeats they endured in 1972 in our country, in Africa and abroad that explain the heightened aggression against our liberated areas, especially in Cubacare which was visited in April by the United Nations Special Mission.

The despair of the fascist Portuguese colonial Government is even more understandable now that it is certain that the "better Guine policy" has totally failed, and it is certain that the lie about a "better Cape Verde" policy will also fail. As far as Guine is concerned, it is the fascist colonial Government in Lisbon itself which, with the voice of the head of the criminal colonial aggressors, confesses to this defeat while stating at the same time that what the African wants is to have "his own political and social voice." It is exactly what the Africans of Guine and Cape Verde Islands wants. But we call that independence, that is to say, the total sovereignty of our people nationally and internationally, to build himself, in peace and dignity through his own efforts and sacrifices, walking on his own two feet and guided by his own head, the progress that is his right, like all the peoples of the world. And this must come about in cooperation with other peoples, including the people of Portugal who, in the course of three liberation wars against Castile or Spain, fought to conquer *their own social and political voice,* their own independence—and won.

Also, as you know, while the populations of the colonialist occupied urban centres show an increasing interest in the Party and the struggles, proved by the great number of young people who have abandoned Bissau and other towns to join the combat, the situation in Portugal is deteriorating with gathering speed and the Portuguese people are voicing their opposition to the colonial war with increasing clamor. The fascist colonial Government in Lisbon and its agents in our country are pressurized into seeking to ascertain whether they can change the situation before their cause becomes completely lost in their own country.

But they are wasting their time and lose the lives of the

young Portuguese they send to war ingloriously and in vain. They will continue to perpetrate crimes against our populace; they will make a lot more attempts at destroying our Party and our struggle. Without a doubt they will take shameless aggressive action against neighboring countries. But all in vain. For no crime, no use of force, no maneuver in word or deed of the criminal Portuguese colonial aggressors will be able to stop the march of history, the irreversible march of our own African people of Guine and the Cape Verde Islands towards their independence.

Forward, comrades and compatriots in the historic struggle for National Liberation! Health, long life and increasing success to our African People, our courageous fighters, to all the militants, organizers and leaders of our great Party!

Let us proclaim the existence of our State in Guine and advance with the victorious struggle of our people in the Cape Verde Islands!

Long live the PAIGC, strength and guide of our people, in Guine and the Cape Verde Islands!

Death to the criminal Portuguese colonial aggressors!

Further Readings

What follows is a survey of selected literature relevant to the life of Amilcar Cabral and the struggle which he led. In this regard it is suggested that the first source a reader should use is the writings of Comrade Cabral himself.

More often than not the plentifulness and depth of Cabral's writings is not pointed out. With this in mind we begin this bibliography suggesting the following additional works by Comrade Cabral.

1. Cabral, Amilcar, "In Defense of the Land"; "Memorandum to the Portuguese Government." Written in 1952 and 1960 respectively, these and other early writings of Cabral can be found (translated into English) in *Emerging Nationalism in Portuguese Africa*, edited by Ronald Chilcote, Stanford, Hoover Institution, 1972. (Though $25.00 this collection is well worth whatever effort is necessary to obtain it. It includes, for example, Cabral's poignant 1961 statement about the "Death Pangs of Imperialism.")

2. Cabral, Amilcar, "The War in Portuguese Guinea," *African Revolution I* (June, 1963) 103-108.

3. Cabral, Amilcar, "The Struggle in Guinea," *International Socialist Journal*, I, (August, 1964) 428-46. This article was reprinted by the Africa Research Group, Cambridge, Mass., in 1969. It is now available from the Africa Information Service.

4. Cabral, Amilcar, "Liberating Portuguese Guinea From Within," *The New African*, IV, (June, 1965) 85. Article

shows how as early as '65 Cabral and the PAIGC regard the liberated areas as having "all the instruments of a state." The interview is conducted by Frene Ginwala, a South African comrade and former editor of the Tanzanian *Standard*.

5. Cabral, Amilcar, "Guinea The Power of Arms" *Triconcontinental* XII, (May-June, 1969) 5-16. This piece provides some elaboration on how the peasantry was mobilized in the early stages of the struggle. It is also available in a good collection of analyses from all the movements in the Portuguese colonies, namely, *Portuguese Colonies: Victory or Death*, Tricontinental, Havana, 1971, 286 pp.

6. Cabral, Amilcar, *Revolution in Guinea: An African People's Struggle, Selected Texts*, Stage I, London, 1969, 142 pp., and *Revolution in Guinea: Selected Texts*, Monthly Review Press, New York, 1970, 174 pp. Both of these are collections of Cabral's speeches and writings.

7. Cabral, Amilcar, "PAIGC: Optimistic and Fighter" *Tricontinental*, Havana, (July-Oct., 1970) 27-29 + 167-74. This is essentially an extract from the June 1970 "Rome Conference in Support of the Peoples of the Portuguese Colonies." The full address by Cabral and the other major addresses are available in *Liberation Struggle in Portuguese Colonies*, All-India Peace Council & Indian Association for Afro-Asian Solidarity, People's Publishing House, New Delhi, 1970, 72 pp.

8. Cabral, Amilcar, "Report on Portuguese Guinea and the Liberation Movement," In *Ufahamu*, Vol. I, No. 2, Univ. of California, Los Angeles (Fall, 1970) 69-103. Full text of Cabral's 1970 appearance before House Subcommittee on African Affairs chaired by Congressman Diggs. On this occasion facing a hostile audience the Secretary General's astuteness and political clarity withers away the Mc Carthy-like questioning coming from subcommittee members like Derwinski of Illinois. The original document (report given February 26, 1970 to the Ninety-First Congress, second session) can be obtained at a nominal fee from the Government Printing Office. The government reprint in-

cludes Cabral's 1969 Report to the Organization of African Unity's Liberation Committee meeting in Dakar, Senegal.

9. Cabral, Amilcar, "A Brief Report on the Situation of the Struggle (Jan.-August 1971)." In *Ufahamu,* Vol. II, No. 3, winter, 1972, pp. 4-25.
10. Cabral, Amilcar, *Our People Are Our Mountains.* Reprint of speech and questions/answers; Central Hall, London, October, 1971, available from Committee for Freedom in Mozambique, Angola and Guine, 12, Little Newport Street, London WC2AH 7 JJ. Very valuable collection of Cabral's recent thoughts and reflections. The questions posed add to the usefulness of this pamphlet.
11. Cabral, Amilcar, "An informal talk by A. Cabral," *Southern Africa* VI, 2 (February 1973) 6-9, published by Southern Africa Committee, 244 W. 27th St., New York 10001.

Much has been written about Comrade Amilcar Cabral. Undoubtedly much more will be written. The following are a few articles which together convey a further impression of our fallen comrade:

12. Ahmed, Feroz, "Amilcar Cabral: An Editorial" *Pakistan Forum, III,* 4 (January, 1973) 3-4 + interview, P.O. Box 1198, Saulte St. Marie, Ont., Canada.
13. Braganca, Aquino, "La Longue Marche d'un Revolutionnaire Africain, "*Afrique Asie,* XXIII, 5 (February 18, 1973) 12-20.
14. Chilcote, Ronald, "The Political Thought of Amilcar Cabral," *Journal of Modern African Studies,* VI, 3, 1968) 373-388.
15. Davidson Basil, "Profile of Amilcar Cabral," *West Africa,* XXVIII (April, 1964).
16. Davidson, Basil, "Cabral's Monument," *New Statesman* (Jan. 26, 1973).
17. Magubane, Bernard, "Amilcar Cabral: Evolution of Revolutionary Thought," *Ufahamu,* II, 2 (Fall, 1971) 71-88.
18. United Nations Office of Public Information, *Objective Justice* (February-March, 1973) issue devoted to Cabral.
19. Reed, Rick, "A Song of World Revolution: In Tribute to Amilcar Cabral," *Institute of the Black World Monthly Re-*

port, February, 1973. 87 Chestnut Street, S.W., Atlanta, Ga. 30314.

20. *Ufahamu,* III, 3 (Winter, 1973 special issue). This issue contains some of Cabral's earliest writings and some good analytical articles. Partial contents: "The Cape Verdeans and the PAIGC Struggle for National Liberation" by Salahudin Matteos—"Theory of Revolution and Background to his Assassination" by Eduardo Ferreira—"Culture and History in a Revolutionary Context" by Maryinez Hubbard—"The PAIGC Without Cabral: An Assessment" by Gerard Chaliand—"Bibliographical Memorial to Amilcar Cabral by Francis Kornegay.

Lastly, and most important, Comrade Cabral must be viewed within the context of the people of Guine and their historical struggle. The following selected books and articles paint an accurate picture of the nature of Portuguese colonialism and the national liberation struggle:

21 Chaliand, Gérard, *Armed Struggle in Africa,* Monthly Review Press, New York, 1969, 142 pp.

22. da Mota, Texeira, *Guinea Portuguesa,* Lisbon, 1954, 2 vols.

23. Davidson, Basil, *The Liberation of Guine: Aspects of an African Revolution,* with a foreword by Amilcar Cabral, Penguin, Baltimore, 1969, 167 pp.

24. Duffy, James, *Portugal in Africa,* Penguin, Baltimore, 1962.

25. Fernandes, Gil, "Talk with a Guinean Revolutionary" *Ufahamu,* I, 1 (Spring, 1970) 6-21. In a frank and concise manner this Guinean comrade of Cabral's describes their struggle giving much information about the revolutionary social transformation underway.

26. Land, Thomas, "Western Investment in Portugal's African Wars" *East African Journal,* University College, Nairobi (June, 1971) 27-29+.

27. Minter, William, *Portuguese Africa and the West,* Penguin, Harmondsworth, England, 1972, 167 pp. and Monthly Review Press, New York, 1973, 200 pp.

28. Rudebeck, Lars, "Political Mobilization in Guinea-Bissau," *Journal of Modern African Studies* (May 1, 1972) 1-18, includes detailed information on the political education program of the PAIGC.

29. United Nations, Office of Public Information, "Mission to Guinea (Bissau)," New York, 1972.